POISONOUS
PYTHONS
PARALYZE
PENNSYLVANIA

Here's what readers from around the country are saying about Johnathan Rand's *AMERICAN CHILLERS:*

"Your books are awesome! I have all the AMERICAN CHILLERS and I keep them right by my bed since I read them every week!"
-*Tommy W, age 9, Michigan*

"My dog chewed up TERRIBLE TRACTORS OF TEXAS, and then he puked. Is that normal?"
-*Carlos V., age 11, New Jersey*

"Johnathan Rand's books are my favorite. They're really creepy and scary!"
-*Jeremy J., age 9, Illinois*

"My whole class loves your books! I have two of them and they are really, really cool."
-*Katie R., age 12, California*

"I never liked to read before, but now I read all the time! The 'Chillers' series is great!"
-*Lauren B., age 10, Ohio*

"I love AMERICAN CHILLERS because they are scary, but not too scary, because I don't want to have nightmares."
-*Adrian P., age 11, Maine*

"I just finished Florida Fog Phantoms. It is a freaky book! I really liked it."
-*Daniel R., Michigan*

"I read all of the books in the MICHIGAN CHILLERS series, and I just started the AMERICAN CHILLERS series. I really love these books!"

-Andrew K., age 13 Montana

"I have six CHILLERS books, and I have read them all three times! I hope I get more for my birthday. My sister loves them, too."

-Jaquann D., age 10, Illinois

"I just read KREEPY KLOWNS OF KALAMAZOO and it really freaked me out a lot. It was really cool!"

-Devin W., age 8, Texas

"THE MICHIGAN MEGA-MONSTERS was great! I hope you write lots more books!"

-Megan P., age 12, Kentucky

"All of my friends love your books! Will you write a book and put my name in it?"

-Michael L., age 10, Ohio

"These books are the best in the world!"

-Garrett M., age 9, Colorado

"We read your books every night. They are really scary and some of them are funny, too."

-Michael & Kristen K., Michigan

"I read THE MICHIGAN MEGA-MONSTERS in two days, and it was cool! When are you going to write one about Wisconsin?"

-John G., age 12, Wisconsin

Look for more'American Chillers®'
from AudioCraft Publishing, Inc.,
coming soon! And don't forget to pick up
these books in Johnathan Rand's thrilling
'Michigan Chillers' series:

#1: Mayhem on Mackinac Island
#2: Terror Stalks Traverse City
#3: Poltergeists of Petoskey
#4: Aliens Attack Alpena
#5: Gargoyles of Gaylord
#6: Strange Spirits of St. Ignace
#7: Kreepy Klowns of Kalamazoo
#8: Dinosaurs Destroy Detroit
#9: Sinister Spiders of Saginaw
#10: Mackinaw City Mummies

American Chillers:
#1: The Michigan Mega-Monsters
#2: Ogres of Ohio
#3: Florida Fog Phantoms
#4: New York Ninjas
#5: Terrible Tractors of Texas
#6: Invisible Iguanas of Illinois
#7: Wisconsin Werewolves
#8: Minnesota Mall Mannequins
#9: Iron Insects Invade Indiana
#10: Missouri Madhouse
#11: Poisonous Pythons Paralyze Pennsylvania

and more coming soon!

AudioCraft Publishing, Inc.
PO Box 281
Topinabee Island, MI 49791

#11: Poisonous Pythons Paralyze Pennsylvania

Johnathan Rand

An AudioCraft Publishing, Inc. book

This book is a work of fiction. Names, places, characters and incidents are used fictitiously, or are products of the author's very active imagination.

Graphics layout/design consultant: Scott Beard, Straits Area Printing
Honorary graphics consultant: Chuck Beard *(we miss you, Chuck)*
Text Prep: Cindee Rocheleau, Sheri Kelley

Book warehouse and storage facilities provided by Clarence and Dorienne's Storage, Car Rental & Shuttle Service, Topinabee Island, MI Security provided by Salty and Abby.

ISBN 1-893699-53-6

Printed in USA
First Printing, August 2003

Poisonous
Pythons
Paralyze
Pennsylvania

VISIT THE OFFICIAL WORLD HEADQUARTERS OF AMERICAN CHILLERS & MICHIGAN CHILLERS!

The all-new HOME for books by Johnathan Rand! Featuring books, hats, shirts, bookmarks and other cool stuff not available anywhere else in the world! Plus, watch the American Chillers website for news of special events and signings at *CHILLERMANIA* with author Johnathan Rand! Located in northern lower Michigan, on I-75 just off exit 313!

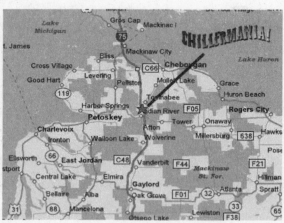

www.americanchillers.com

1

"See anything yet?" I called out.

"Nothing yet," I heard a voice in the woods reply. The voice belonged to my friend Stephen Kottler. We were hunting for garter snakes in the woods near our house. So far, we hadn't found anything, and I was about to give up.

My name is Ryan Brindley, and I live in Maple Glen. It's a city in Pennsylvania, not far from Philadelphia. We used to live in Missouri, but we moved here a few years ago when Mom changed jobs. I really like it here. There are lots of forests and trees, but best of all . . . garter snakes.   Garter snakes are my favorite kind of snake. First of all, you can find them just about anywhere. They are black with a yellow stripe down their back, and they have a creamy yellow belly. Plus, they're pretty much harmless. Oh, I caught a lot of garter snakes when I lived in Missouri, but I catch more here.

We don't really do anything with the snakes, either. I used to think that it would be cool to have one as a pet, but you can't keep a wild snake. I think it's more fun just to catch a snake and watch it for a while and then let it go.

My friend Stephen loves to catch snakes, too, and so does our friend Heather Lewis. I used to think that girls didn't like snakes, but Heather does, and she's good at catching them, too. Today, she had soccer practice, so she couldn't be with us.

And normally, we all have a lot of fun.
Normally.

But today, we would discover something that would turn our entire city upside down.

"Let's hunt in the swamp," I suggested, and pretty soon I saw Stephen appear from the woods. His blonde hair shone in the afternoon sun, and his face was damp with sweat.

"Yeah, let's try the swamp," he agreed. "I haven't seen a single snake."

The swamp isn't far from where we live. It's dense and thick, and it's hard to walk through.

We had just entered the swamp. I was right behind Stephen when suddenly, he stopped.

"Shhh," he said. "I thought I heard something."

Quietly, I stepped up to his side. We listened. All we could hear were a few birds chirping, and the sound of a small airplane way up in the sky.

And suddenly—

We heard it.

The crackling, swishing sounds that a snake makes as it moves through brush and branches.

But this sound was different, somehow. It sounded . . .

Heavier.

Bigger.

If it was a snake, it was a big one.

My heart pounded. *"I think it's over there somewhere,"* I said, raising my arm to point.

Carefully, we took a few steps forward.

"There!" Stephen pointed. "I saw something move!"

We sprang, unaware that what we were about to find wasn't just some ordinary garter snake.

Now, I'm not afraid of snakes.

Period.

But what I saw that day was *horrifying*.

2

My heart stopped. Well, not really . . . but that's what it felt like. Stephen screamed. I thought for a moment he was going to pass out.

It was a snake, all right . . . but it was like no snake I had ever seen in my life.

First of all, it was *big*. Longer than a car. It had splotches of different colors—green, gray, brown, and black.

And it was as big around as a football.

We couldn't move. We scarcely dared to breathe. Much less *do* something. There was no way we were going to even *think* about catching this snake.

And besides . . . it's not smart to catch just any snake you see. Some of them bite, but I've found that if you leave them alone, they'll leave you alone. So it's not a good idea to just catch any snake that you come across. That's just asking for trouble.

"What . . . what kind of snake is that?" Stephen gulped.

"It looks like some kind of boa constrictor," I answered quietly. *"But I can't be sure."*

"But there aren't any boa constrictors in Maple Glen, let alone Pennsylvania!" Stephen said.

The snake wasn't doing much, and it didn't seem to pay much attention to us. Finally, after a few more moments, it slowly slithered off into the swamp. The snake was gone.

"That was too cool!" I shouted after the snake had disappeared.

"That was awesome!" Stephen cried. "I've never seen a snake that big in my life!"

It was really kind of cool to see a snake like that, so close to home.

But something really bothered me.

That snake, whatever it was, wasn't from Pennsylvania. True, there are several kinds of snakes in our state—but none that grow to the size of the snake we'd seen in the swamp.

Later, when I got home, I looked through all of my snake books. I have lots of books on snakes, and I read all about them all the time. I tried to find the name of the snake we'd spotted, but I couldn't find this snake in any of my books. I found a lot that looked like it, but I couldn't find the *exact* snake.

So I decided that I would go back into the swamp and see if I could find the snake again. I knew that Stephen would want to go, too.

I went to bed and fell asleep, not knowing that the very next day would lead to a discovery—a discovery that everyone in Maple Glen and even the entire state of Pennsylvania would never forget.

3

I got up early the next morning, and made preparations. I placed a couple of my snake books in my backpack, along with a first-aid kit, a ball of string, some mosquito repellent, and a compass—just in case we got lost in the swamp.

Then I rode my bike over to Stephen's house. He only lives a few blocks away.

Stephen was waiting in the garage. He had a backpack, too, but he was also carrying bottles of water and sandwiches that his mom had made for us.

"All set?" I asked.

"Let's go snake hunting!" he said excitedly.

Our plan was to ride down to a small park that bordered on the edge of the swamp. From there, we could enter the swamp quickly without having to hike though the forest. Plus, we would ride right past Heather Lewis' house. I was sure she would want to go with us today!

We stopped at her house and rang the doorbell. The door opened, and her mother appeared.

"Hi Mrs. Lewis," I said. "Is Heather around?"

"I'm afraid she's visiting her grandparents," Mrs. Lewis said. "But she'll be home later. I'll let her know you stopped by."

"Wait until she finds out what she missed!" Stephen said as we hopped on our bikes and rode out of the driveway.

"I sure hope we see that monster snake again," I said.

We rode down the block. In no time at all, we were at the park. We locked our bikes up around a tree.

"Time to find us a snake," I said as we entered the swamp.

"A *giant* snake!" Stephen chimed in.

"With *huge* teeth!" I exclaimed.

"And dark, beady eyes!" Stephen said.

We were excited, for sure.

But after hours and hours of scouring the swamp, we hadn't seen any evidence of the enormous snake. I caught one garter snake, and I let him go after a few minutes.

But that was all.

At noon, we decided to split up. We'd have a better chance finding the snake if we could each cover a little more ground. Every few minutes we would call out, just to make sure that we didn't get too far away from each other.

Branches scratched at my face. My muscles ached. Mosquitos nipped at my arm, even though I had bug spray on.

Man, I thought. *There is no way we're going to find that thing.*

I was bummed. I was really hoping that we'd see the snake again, but I knew that our chances were slim.

And suddenly. . . .

"HOLY COW!"

Stephen's voice pierced the swamp.

"Are you okay?" I called out frantically.

"Ryan! Get over here! You've got to see this!"

"Is it the snake?" I yelled back. I was already headed in his direction, sweeping branches and brush out of my way.

"You're not going to believe this!" Stephen shouted. *"You're going to freak out!"*

And when I arrived at his side, I gasped.

Stephen was wrong.

When I saw what he'd found, I didn't just freak out.

I went bananas.

4

Stephen had found a snake skin.

Not just any snake skin.

An *enormous* snake skin.

You see, every once in a while, a snake will shed its skin. It rubs up against branches and brush, and the old skin gets caught. Then it kind of wriggles out, leaving behind a skin that is thin, like plastic. The shed skin is usually a creamy, light-brown color. It dries and becomes very brittle, but what it looks like, really, is the ghost of the snake. You can see the texture of scales on the skin and everything. I've found a few snake skins over the summer.

But none like this one.

Stephen and I just stared. The snake skin that we'd found must have been from the snake we saw the day before, because the skin was *huge.*

"I can't believe it!" Stephen whispered.

"Man, Heather is going to be sorry she missed finding this!" I said.

But we also knew something else:

The snake, wherever it was, might be dangerous.

"We have to tell someone," I said.

"Who?" Stephen replied. "The police?"

"No," I said, shaking my head. "We have to tell someone who knows about snakes. Someone who might know what kind of snake it is."

"But who?" Stephen said, as he scratched his head.

We thought and thought about it. The entire time, we didn't take our eyes off the giant snake skin.

All of a sudden, I knew who we could talk to.

"The pet store!" I exclaimed. "They have all kinds of different animals, including snakes! I'll bet the guy who runs the pet store would know what kind of snake this is!"

"Good idea!" Stephen replied. "But how are we going to get this skin out of here?"

"We're not," I said. "We'll leave it here. We'll bring the owner of the pet store out here to see it."

"Suppose we can't find it again?" Stephen asked.

"I've already got that one figured out," I said, as I slipped my backpack off. I unzipped it and pulled out the ball of string. "See? I'll tie this string onto this branch—"

As I spoke, I wound the string around a small sapling.

"—And I'll just let it out as we walk back. When we come back, all we have to do is follow the string. It'll lead us right to the snake skin!"

"Ryan, you're a genius!" Stephen shouted, and he raised his hand in the air. I slapped it and then bowed.

"Yes, I am, aren't I?" I said with a smirk. "Come on. If we hurry, we can get to the pet store before it closes."

We backtracked through the swamp. All the while, I was letting out string so that we could follow it right back to the snake skin.

And I couldn't wait to tell the pet store owner! I was sure he'd be excited to see it.

Going back through the swamp was even more difficult than it was coming in. I had to go slower to let out the string. In many places the brush was so thick that I couldn't even see my shoes. Still, we pressed on, pushing branches and limbs out of our way as we moved forward.

We were almost out of the swamp. I was excited about going to the pet store and telling the owner about what we had found. He would know more about the snake skin, I was sure.

And so, I wasn't really paying attention to where I was walking. I was thinking about giant snakes and snake skins and—

Suddenly, I felt two sharp pains in my lower leg. It hurt! I screamed and tried to get away, but it was already too late. . . .

5

The sharp pain in my leg made me cry out. When I looked down, I could immediately see the problem.

"Hornets!" I shrieked, and I began scrambling through the swamp faster than ever. I thrashed through the thick brush, desperately trying to get away.

"Yeeouch!" Stephen yelped. He'd been stung, too!

We kept flailing and scrambling through the swamp. I was too afraid to stop. We'd stepped on a nest of hornets, and I knew from experience that they'd swarm and come after us. Hornets are nothing to mess around with, that's for sure.

After a few minutes of clumsy running, we stopped. I didn't see any of the hornets coming after us, and I figured that we were far enough away from their nest.

"That hurt!" Stephen said, wincing and rubbing his arm. He had a big red welt where the hornet had stung him. He also had a few long red lines from where branches had scraped him.

I bent over and rolled up my pant leg. The two hornets had stung me just above the ankle, and there were two marble-sized lumps.

"Man!" I exclaimed. "When I first felt that sting, I thought I'd been bitten by the giant snake! I was freaked!"

"We're just lucky we got away," Stephen said, still rubbing his arm.

We continued walking. Suddenly, Stephen stopped.

"The string!" he said. "What happened to it?!?!"

"I dropped it back by the nest of hornets," I replied. "But don't worry. We're close enough to the park now. I think we can make our way around the hornets' nest and find the string. After all, we're really not far from the snake skin. It just takes longer going through the thick brush."

We came to the edge of the swamp. I could see our bikes, still locked to the tree where we'd left them.

"Come on," I said, jogging to the tree. "Let's ride over to the pet store right now!"

We pedaled through the side streets and then into the downtown area. The pet store was right in the middle of town, on the corner. I hopped off my bike and leaned it against the building, and Stephen followed suit.

But when I opened the door, I knew instantly that something was wrong.

There, face down on the floor, was the pet store owner! Something had happened to him!

6

His arms were outstretched, and one of them was under the counter.

And right next to him, on the tile floor, was a black snake, all coiled up.

The pet store owner had been bitten!

"We've got to get some help!" I exclaimed. "We have to call an ambulance!"

Suddenly, the pet store owner moved! He rolled over to his side and looked at us. He had dark hair and a thick beard and mustache. His glasses had slid down his nose, and he pushed them back into place with a single finger.

"Why?" he said. "Are you hurt?"

"Not me," I said. "You are!" I pointed at the snake on the floor next to him. "That thing bit you!"

He looked at the black snake, reached over, and picked it up.

"Who, Harry?" he said, looking at the snake. "Why, he wouldn't hurt a fly . . . unless he was hungry."

"But we thought you were hurt," Stephen said. "We saw you on the floor like that, and then we saw the snake, and we thought that you'd been bitten."

"Not at all," the man replied. "I was carrying Harry back to his cage, when I dropped my keys." He held up a ring that dangled several silver and gold keys. "They fell under the counter. I had to crawl on the floor to reach them."

Boy, did I feel silly.

"Give me a minute," the man said. "I'll put Harry back in his cage, and I'll be back to help you."

We were still standing at the door of the pet store, so we walked inside. We saw birds chirping from cages, and aquariums bubbling. Inside the aquariums were fish of all different sizes and colors. On one wall was a row of glass cases that had several different creatures: tarantulas, lizards, snakes . . . even turtles. On the opposite wall were wire cages that held gerbils, hamsters, guinea pigs, and small bunnies.

The man returned. "Well, then. What can I help you gentlemen with?"

"A snake!" I said excitedly.

The man's eyes lit up. "Ah! My specialty. I love snakes, and I have several to choose from." He began walking toward a row of glass cases.

"No, no," Stephen said. "We don't *want* any snake. We found a snake skin—"

"—a *huge* one!" I interjected.

"—in the swamp!" Stephen finished.

The man stroked his beard and frowned. "Just how big?" he asked.

"Longer than a car!" I exclaimed, spreading my arms wide.

"It's gigantic!" Stephen said, and he, too, spread his arms wide.

"That's interesting," the man said, still stroking his beard. "Tell me . . . where did you find this skin?"

"Down in the swamp," I answered. "We saw a huge snake yesterday, and we went back to look for it today."

"We didn't find the snake," Stephen added, "but we found its skin."

The pet store owner looked up, as if gazing into space. "The swamp," he said. "That's not far from the college."

He was right, of course. There is a small community college located not too far from the swamp.

The man looked at me, then at Stephen. "Do you still have the skin?" he asked.

I shook my head. "We didn't touch it," I replied. "We figured you might want to see it. I knew if we tried to bring it out of the swamp, we would probably tear it."

"Wise decision," the pet store owner said. "Do you think you could locate it again? I would be very interested in seeing it."

"Sure," I replied. "We could take you right to it."

The pet store owner looked over at the clock. "I have to work until five o'clock, then I'll close the store. Will you meet me at the park after that?"

We nodded in unison.

"Great!" the man said. "Oh. By the way—" he extended his hand, and I took it. "My name is Mr. Larson," he said.

"I'm Ryan," I said. "And this is my friend, Stephen."

He shook Stephen's hand and smiled.

"Nice to meet both of you," he said. "I'll see you later today."

We left the store and hung out around town for a while. When five o'clock came, we pedaled back to the park. Moments later, Mr. Larson drove up in a shiny black van.

"Ready?" he said.

"Let's go," I said, and the three of us entered the swamp. I was a little leery of running into those hornets again, so I made a wide circle around them and was able to locate the string.

"Here we go," I said. "We're not far away at all."

We followed the string until we reached the point where I had tied it to a branch.

But something was very wrong.

The snake skin was missing!

7

"I . . . I don't understand," I stammered. "It was right here!"

"Are you sure we're in the right spot?" Mr. Larson asked.

"Positive," I said. "I tied the string to this branch so we would be able to find our way back."

The three of us were silent for a moment. Stephen and I looked all around, but there was no sign of the snake skin.

"Are you sure you found a snake skin?" Mr. Larson asked.

He didn't believe us!

"Honest, Mr. Larson," Stephen said. "It was right here. We're not lying. There was a huge snake skin right here!"

"Well, it's gone now," Mr. Larson said. He turned. "I've got a lot of things to do. If you boys come across this giant snake, let me know."

I could tell by his voice that he didn't believe we'd seen the snake, and he certainly didn't believe that we'd found a giant snake skin.

The three of us traipsed through the dense swamp until we were back at the park. Mr. Larson didn't say much more. He just got into his van and left.

"I don't understand," I said. "That snake skin was right there. How could it have gone anywhere?"

"Maybe someone else found it," Stephen said.

I shook my head. "Not many people go into the swamp besides us," I said.

We stood at the edge of the swamp for a moment. I looked at my watch.

"I have to go home for supper soon," I said. "But I want to have another look."

"In the swamp?" Stephen replied.

"Of course," I said. "Stephen, that snake skin has got to be there somewhere. Maybe it got dragged off by some animal or something."

"Maybe the snake got cold and came back for it," Stephen said.

"Yeah, right," I said, rolling my eyes. "Come on."

"All right," Stephen said. "But not for too long. I have to be home for supper soon, too."

And so, for the third time that day, we entered the swamp.

This time, however, was different.

This time, we were being watched.

We just didn't know it yet.

8

We followed the string back to where the snake skin should have been, being careful not to get close to the spot where the hornets' nest was. I wanted to leave those little buggers alone.

"Let's split up and circle around this area," I said. We searched and searched, but we didn't see any sign of the snake skin. I couldn't believe that it had simply vanished into thin air.

Where could it be? Had an animal run off with it? If it did, I'm sure pieces of the skin would have broken off and we would have found them.

It just didn't make sense.

"Hey Ryan," Stephen called out. He wasn't very far away, but in the thick of the swamp, I couldn't see him.

"Over here," I called back. "Did you find it?"

"Nope. But it's getting close to my supper time. If I'm late again, Dad's going to go bananas."

"Yeah, we should go," I said reluctantly. I turned around and trudged back to the spot where we had originally found the snake skin. In a moment, Stephen appeared, pushing branches out of his way. He had leaves in his hair and on his shirt.

"You look like you've been rolling around on the ground," I said.

"Hey, you don't look much better," he said. "You have twigs in your hair and your shirt is ripped."

Great. How would I explain that to Mom?

We followed the string through the swamp. When we came close to where the hornets' nest was, we went way around it.

"Want to try again tomorrow?" I asked.

Stephen didn't answer, but he stopped walking.

"Well?" I asked again. "Whaddya say? Want to come back again tomorrow?"

"Shhh!" Stephen replied, placing a finger to his lips. Then he pointed. *"I just saw something move over there."*

We froze in our tracks. Suddenly, a branch moved! The motion was very slight, but it was obvious that *something* made it move.

But the branches and leaves were so thick, we couldn't see what it was.

"It's that snake we saw yesterday," Stephen said. "I'm sure of it."

The branch wiggled again, but we still couldn't see what was causing it to move.

Carefully, I took a step toward the thick branches. Stephen followed for a few steps, then we stopped. Right in front of us, the branches rustled again. I tried to peer through the leaves but it was no use. I couldn't see anything.

"On the count of three, let's grab the branches and pull them," I whispered. Stephen nodded, and we readied ourselves by reaching our arms out.

"*One . . . two . . . THREE!*"

We sprang, grabbed the branches, and pulled them apart . . . and were instantly attacked!

9

We did the only thing we could do—scream! Suddenly, Stephen recognized our attacker. His face turned red with embarrassment.

"Heather!" Stephen cried. "You freaked us out!"

"Good!" she replied with a laugh. "It's about time I got you guys back!"

Heather Lewis is tall. Tall and slender. She has long brown hair, and today it was speckled with dry leaves from the swamp.

"When did you get here?" I asked.

"A little while ago. Mom said you guys stopped by, and I thought you'd be here in the swamp. Find anything?"

"Did we *ever!*" I exclaimed, and Stephen and I told her about how we'd seen the giant snake the day before, and about the snake skin. We told her about Mr. Larson, and how we brought him out to the swamp, only to find that the skin was gone.

"Was he the man that was with you guys a little while ago?" Heather asked. "A guy with a thick beard and glasses?"

Stephen and I nodded. "That's him," I said. "He's a really nice guy, but I think he thinks we were trying to fool him."

"You know," Heather said, picking a leaf from her hair. "He was in the swamp earlier today."

"What?!?!" I replied.

"Mr. Larson?!?!" said Stephen.

"Yeah," Heather said. "It was a while ago, though. I came to the park to look for you guys, and I saw a man come out of the swamp carrying a big bag. He put it in a black van and took off."

I was stunned. "That was him!" I said. "It had to be!" I turned and looked at Stephen. "While we were in town waiting for five o'clock to roll around, Mr. Larson came out here and took our snake skin!"

"Then he came back here with us, and of course the skin was gone!" Stephen piped in.

I was confused. "Why would he do that?" I wondered aloud. "Why would he come and take the snake skin and not tell us?"

"Sounds like he's got something to hide," Heather said, still picking leaves out of her hair.

"Let's go back to the pet store and talk to him tomorrow morning," I said angrily. "I want to know what's going on, and why he would do that."

"I'm in," Stephen said.

"Don't leave me out," Heather said.

So that was what we would do. In the morning, we would ride our bikes downtown to the pet store and talk to Mr. Larson. We would talk to him, and we would find out why he had taken the snake skin.

Of course, we didn't know it at the time, but we would find out a lot more than that. Even now, I shudder as I remember what happened that morning . . . .

10

"But it can't be closed," Stephen said.

The three of us had our faces pressed against the glass of the pet store window. Just as we had agreed, we rode our bikes together into town in the morning. The pet store should have already been open . . . but it wasn't.

I read the sign on the door. "It says the store opens at nine a.m.," I said, "but it's almost ten."

Again, I peered through the window. We could see all of the cages and tanks and aquariums clearly, but there were no lights on.

And Mr. Larson was nowhere to be found.

"Well, let's wait a little longer and see if he shows up," I said. "Maybe he wasn't feeling well this morning."

"Yeah," Stephen said bitingly. "Maybe he feels guilty for swiping our snake skin."

We waited around for about a half an hour, but we still didn't see any sign of Mr. Larson.

Then, Stephen got an idea.

"Hey," he said. "Let's go around back. Let's see if there's anything back there."

I didn't think we'd find much of anything, but it was worth a shot.

We walked down the block until we came to an alley. Then we turned and walked down the alley until it wound behind a row of buildings.

"Look!" Heather cried. She raised her arm and pointed. "There's his van!"

She was right! Mr. Larson's black van was parked behind the pet store. There was also a big truck with a trailer parked next to it. Next to the truck was a smaller blue car.

"Maybe that's why he hasn't opened the store," I said. "He's been busy unloading stuff."

"Let's go find out," Stephen said, and we continued walking behind the buildings, getting closer and closer to the black van and the truck with the trailer.

We had almost reached the van when we heard voices.

"Quick!" I whispered. "Duck down!"

The three of us hunkered down on the side of the van, out of sight. From where we were, we could hear the two men talking, but we weren't close enough to understand what they were saying. Soon, the other man got into the blue car and left, and Mr. Larson turned and walked into the pet store from the rear entrance.

"Come on!" I said, and I stood up. Heather and Stephen followed, and we crept around the side of the van and looked around.

"Would you recognize that bag again if you saw it?" I asked Heather.

She nodded. "Yeah," she said. "I know I would."

We didn't see the black bag anywhere, or any evidence of the snake skin. He probably had it in the pet store.

51

"I'll bet he's going to sell it," Stephen fumed. "That's why he took it and didn't tell us. He's probably going to make a fortune!"

"Calm down," I said. "I doubt that an old snake skin is worth any money. If anything, he'll probably put it somewhere in his store for people to see. Come on. Let's go talk to him!"

"Wait!" Heather exclaimed. "Look at that! Look what's written on those crates in the trailer!"

Ryan and I turned, and stared in disbelief at what we saw.

11

Stephen and I read the words together, out loud.

"DANGER—POISONOUS SNAKES."

"Poisonous snakes!?!?" I repeated. "That's whacked out!"

"I wonder where they came from?" Heather said.

"I wonder where they're going?" Stephen countered.

Inside the trailer that was connected to the truck were dozens of crates. All of them were stamped with the words DANGER—POISONOUS SNAKES.

I raised my foot and stepped up into the trailer.

"Ryan," Heather said. She turned around and looked at the back door of the pet shop. "I don't think that's a good idea."

"Relax," I said. "I'm not going to take anything. I just want to check this out."

"Me too," Stephen said. "I've never been this close to a bunch of poisonous snakes before!"

The crates were sealed, but they had small holes for air.

"Listen!" I said. *"You can hear them moving around!"*

Now Heather was interested, and she stepped up into the trailer. We listened.

All around us, we could hear the snakes moving in their crates. Far in the back, I heard the unmistakable sound of a rattlesnake shaking its tail.

We walked deeper into the trailer, listening to the snakes. I sure wished that I could see them!

Suddenly, we heard a sound that we definitely did *not* want to hear:

The back door of the pet store opening! Mr. Larson was coming!

"Quick!" I said. *"Behind the crates!"*

In a flash, we ducked down and hid behind the stacked crates of poisonous snakes.

We could hear footsteps approaching the trailer. My heart was beating a mile a minute!

We heard gravel crunching close to the trailer, and then we heard a loud squeak.

Then, we heard the sound that sent a wave of terror through my body:

The trailer door! The trailer door was closing!

And before we knew it—*slam!* The door was closed. Everything was dark. I mean *inky* black. I couldn't see a thing.

We heard several loud clunks as the trailer door was secured. Then the only thing we heard was the sound of snakes slithering in their crates.

It was then that I realized what had happened.

We were locked in the trailer.

In total darkness.

With hundreds of poisonous snakes!

12

I leaped to my feet, and bumped into Stephen. "Easy!" I said. "We don't want to knock any of these crates over!"

Slowly, we made our way to the door. It was so dark that we couldn't see a single thing, and I actually ran right into the trailer door.

Then I started pounding. So did Stephen and Heather.

"Hey! We're in here! Let us out! Let us out!"

I was sure that Mr. Larson would hear us. I was also sure that we'd probably get into trouble, but right now, that didn't really matter. The only thing that mattered was getting out of the trailer.

We pounded and shouted, but no one came.

And then—

Another sound.

The sound of a truck starting.

We were moving!

"Sit down!" Heather said. "So we don't fall down and hit the crates!"

The three of us fell to the floor of the trailer. I couldn't believe this was happening!

"Where are we going?" Stephen asked.

"I have no idea," I replied. "But we're on our way."

"Guys," Heather said in the darkness. "This could be serious. I mean . . . this truck and trailer might be on its way to some zoo a thousand miles away!"

"I hope you're wrong," I replied.

We went over a bump, and all of the crates bounced around.

"We've got to think of something," Stephen said. "If I have to call my mom from a thousand miles away and have her come get me, I'll be grounded until I'm grandpa's age!"

"We'll have to wait until the truck stops," I said. "Then we'll have to get Mr. Larson's attention."

And so, we would have to wait. We would have to just stay cool, keep our heads, and wait for the truck to stop.

The trailer hit another bump, sending a jolt through the trailer. I could still hear snakes slithering in their crates. Rattlesnakes shook their tails in anger.

All of a sudden, the trailer hit a bump so hard that it sent us in the air several inches! I landed with a thud.

But that wasn't the worst part.

The worst part came from the back of the trailer.

We heard a loud crash, and a splintering of wood, and we knew that it could only mean one thing.

One of the crates had fallen.

It had fallen . . . and broken.

We were trapped in the trailer, in darkness, with hundreds of poisonous snakes in wood crates—and one live one, slithering about on the floor of the trailer.

Things were *definitely* not going our way.

13

"Don't anybody move," I said quietly. "Not a muscle."

This was a nightmare. Actually, it was worse. I've never had a nightmare that was as bad as this.

"Do . . . do you think a snake got loose?" Heather peeped.

"I have no idea," I said. "But I heard a crate break."

"It's probably a king cobra or a black mamba," Stephen said.

"You're a big help," I said.

"Well, cobras are poisonous. So are mambas. All of these snakes are poisonous."

"Let's just hope that it stays at its end of the trailer," Heather said.

"And remember not to move," I said. "If we don't move, maybe it'll leave us alone."

I was totally freaked out. My heart was pounding so hard, I thought it was going to bust out of my chest. I tried to calm myself down.

It's going to be fine, I told myself. *It's all going to be fine.*

The truck slowed. We grew hopeful, thinking that maybe the truck was stopping.

No luck. I could feel it go around a sharp turn, and then it sped up again.

Without warning, the truck hit another bump, sending the trailer bouncing up again.

And suddenly, Stephen was screaming.

"A snake! It's right by me! I felt it by my arm! Aaaahhhhhhhhh!"

14

It was total chaos and confusion.

"It's the snake!" Stephen shrieked. *"The poisonous snake is right here!"*

And what made it worse, of course, is that it was too dark to see anything.

"Wait a minute!" Stephen shouted. *"I've got it! I've got it right by the head!"*

"Owwwwwwch!" Heather squealed. *"That's not a snake . . . that's my arm! Let me go!"*

"Your arm?!?!" Stephen said. "I thought it was the poisonous snake trying to bite me!"

"You're lucky it wasn't," Heather said. "That snake would have bitten you for sure, you scaredy-cat."

"I'm not a scaredy-cat!" Stephen insisted.

"You are too!"

"Am not!"

"Both of you guys!" I said. "Knock it off! That snake could be anywhere!"

That got them quiet again. The thought of a poisonous snake loose in the trailer was enough to make them forget about name-calling.

And then, to our complete joy, the truck slowed, and slowed some more—

And stopped!

We heard the engine shut off, and a door close. Too afraid to move, we just sat there on the floor and shouted.

"Help! Let us out of here! Let us out!"

But nobody came!

We yelled and yelled, and waited and waited, but nobody came.

"This is crazy," Heather said. "We've got to get out of here!"

"But the snake!" Stephen said. "What if it's right next to you at this very second?"

"What if it was killed when the crate hit the floor?" Heather said. I could hear movement, and I knew that Heather had stood up. She pounded on the door.

"Hey! If anyone can hear this, there's someone in here! Hey! Anybody!"

She pounded for a moment, and then stopped. I heard a metal rattling sound.

"Ryan! Stephen!" she shouted excitedly. *"Give me a hand! Guess what I found?!?!"*

15

"What is it?" I asked nervously, as I rose to my feet. I still wasn't sure if there was a poisonous snake loose or not.

"I think it's a door lever," Heather answered, and again, I heard the metal rattling sound. "Help me lift it."

I fumbled in the darkness until I found the lever.

"Let's try pushing it down," I said. After struggling with it for a moment, we stopped.

"Okay," Heather said. "Let's try lifting it up."

We grunted and groaned as we struggled to lift up the lever, but it was no use.

"You've got the wrong idea," Stephen said. "My dad has a trailer like this. There's a lever inside, but there's a pin that locks it tight."

"You're just now telling us this?!?!" Heather snapped.

I heard Stephen moving, then I felt his hands on mine.

"Move your hands," he said. I withdrew my hands from the lever. I could hear him fumbling with something for a minute, and then he stopped.

"Now try it," he said. "Lift the lever up."

Heather and I grasped the lever and lifted. Suddenly, the door swung open and daylight flooded the trailer. I don't think I had ever been so happy in my entire life.

We cheered as the door opened, but not for very long.

Because it was then that we saw the two figures, standing behind the trailer . . . waiting for us.

And I'll say this much: they didn't look happy.

16

The two figures just stared as the trailer door opened. One of the men was Mr. Larson, and the other was the man that we'd seen at the pet store a little while ago—the same man who had left in the blue car.

"What on earth?!?!" Mr. Larson exclaimed. We said nothing in response. We were too busy scrambling out of the truck. After all, there was a poisonous snake loose in the trailer!

We hopped down, and the three of us started talking all at once. Mr. Larson raised his hand.

"Please, one at a time, one at a time. First of all, are you children all right?"

"Fine," I said.

"Yeah, me too," Stephen said.

"My arm hurts where Stephen grabbed it," Heather said. "He thought it was a snake."

"It could have been!" Stephen protested.

"How on earth did you get into this trailer?" Mr. Larson asked.

"We were looking at the crates of snakes," I explained. "We accidentally got locked in here."

"You mean . . . you rode in this trailer all the way from the pet store?" the other man gasped.

"Yeah," Stephen said. "It sure was a bumpy ride."

"One of the crates fell and broke," I said. "I think there's a snake loose."

The two men sprang into action. First, they leaned into the trailer to inspect the damage. Sure enough, there was a crate near the front of the trailer that had fallen over.

"I don't think it's broken badly enough for the snake to escape," Mr. Larson said. He climbed into the trailer and cautiously made his way to the broken crate.

"He's okay," he said. "The snake is still inside the crate. I don't think it's hurt."

"Yeah, well, *we* didn't know that," Stephen said. "We were freaking out."

"*You* were freaking out," Heather said, and she poked him in the ribs.

"But why did you take the snake skin?" I asked, looking at Mr. Larson. "I know you did, because Heather saw you. She saw you come out of the swamp with a black bag. You had the snake skin in that bag, didn't you?"

Mr. Larson looked at the other man. "I have to tell them," he said to him.

The other man looked pained. "I don't think it is a good idea," he said.

"But they need to know. I betrayed their trust, and I must tell them why."

The other man sighed. "If you must," he said.

And with that, Mr. Larson turned to us and began to explain . . . and let me tell you, what he said was so bizarre—so freaky—that I had a hard time believing it.

17

"First of all," Mr. Larson began, "please allow me to apologize. Yes, it was I who removed the snake skin from the swamp."

"I *knew* it!" Stephen cried.

"Shhh!" said Heather.

"Secondly, let me introduce Mr. Plumbody. He is an expert herpetologist here at the college."

For the first time, I looked around, and realized that we hadn't traveled very far, after all. The college isn't that far from our house, and, as a matter of fact, the swamp where we hunt for snakes is on the other side of the college.

"What's a herpergolly . . . a hepatigist . . . I mean—"

"A herpetologist," Mr. Plumbody corrected. "A herpetologist is someone who studies reptiles and amphibians. You know . . . snakes and frogs and turtles. But mostly, I study snakes. And the snake you saw a couple of days ago in the swamp—"

"—the huge one?" I asked.

"Yes," Mr. Plumbody continued. "That snake was one I've been studying in my laboratory. Somehow, it got loose. I had no idea where it'd gone . . . until Mr. Larson called me after you paid him a visit yesterday. I was certain that it was my missing snake. My team and I scoured the swamp, and we were able to find the snake and return it to my laboratory."

"I went to the area in the swamp to find the snake skin before anyone else, and I removed it and brought it to Mr. Plumbody."

"But why?" I asked. "Why did you take it?"

"We didn't want word to get out that the snake was loose," Mr. Plumbody said. "Although the particular snake that was missing is a harmless snake, it might have caused a lot of panic in the city. Mr. Larson removed the snake skin and gave it to me, in case anyone else found it and reported it."

I guess I understood. I imagine a lot of people would have been pretty uptight if they thought that a fifteen-foot snake was loose near their house, regardless of whether it was harmless or not.

"But what about all of these poisonous snakes?" I asked. "What are you doing with these?"

"I study poisonous snakes," Mr. Plumbody said. "Actually, I study the snake's venom. We try to learn about it, and try to find an antidote that will counter the effects of the poison."

"What's an antidote?" Stephen asked.

"An antidote, in this instance, would be a cure," Mr. Plumbody explained. "So that if someone was accidentally bitten by a poisonous snake, and we had an antidote, it may save their life."

"I'll bet you have a lot of cool snakes in your laboratory!" I said.

"Would you like to see it?" Mr. Plumbody asked. "I have many unusual and exotic snakes."

My jaw about hit the floor.

"I'd *love* to see it!" I exclaimed.

"Me too!" said Heather.

"Yeah, cool!" Stephen said.

"I'll tell you what," Mr. Plumbody said. "Come to the college tomorrow evening. Just go to the main office, and I will leave three visitor passes for you. I will give you a tour of my laboratory and show you all of the snakes that we have."

I couldn't wait! We were going to see some of the coolest snakes on the planet! It was a dream come true.

Little did I know that tomorrow night, I would wish that it had only been a dream.

But it wouldn't be. It would be real.

Maple Glen—and all of Pennsylvania—was about to experience a night of slithering terror.

18

I was so excited when I went to bed that night I could hardly sleep. I've always loved snakes, and now I was going to see many different kinds, real close-up. Maybe I would even be able to hold some of the nonpoisonous ones!

The next morning, I rode my bike over to Stephen's house. Stephen was in the garage looking at a magazine.

"Check this out!" he said, and he showed me a page.

"What is it?" I asked.

"Look here. It's a fake rubber snake! See how real it looks?"

I looked at the magazine ad. The snake was big, and it sure did look real.

"I ordered it a couple of weeks ago," Stephen said. "It should be here any day now."

"Man, you'll be able to freak some people out with that!" I exclaimed.

"You bet!" Stephen said. "I can hardly wait."

I had lunch at Stephen's house. We goofed around most of the day, playing catch and shooting hoops. Finally, I went home for supper.

I was so excited that mom had to tell me twice to eat slower. She said I was going to choke if I didn't slow down.

After supper, I rode my bike back over to Stephen's house and the two of us rode over to get Heather. From there, the three of us would ride along the street that wound around the park, until we finally reached the college. It wouldn't take us very long at all.

We chattered excitedly as we rode, trying to imagine what kind of snakes Mr. Plumbody had in his laboratory.

"I'll bet he has giant anacondas!" Stephen said.

"Maybe," I said. "I'm sure he has lots of different kinds."

"I wonder how that one particular snake got loose," Heather said. "I mean . . . that's a big snake. I wonder how it actually got out of the lab and found its way to the swamp."

"Maybe someone was taking it for a walk and it broke the leash," Stephen snickered. Heather just rolled her eyes.

"Well, the swamp isn't far from the college," I said. "It would seem like the best place for the snake to hide."

"Could you imagine what would happen if a bunch of snakes got loose?" Stephen said. "A bunch of poisonous ones? That would be freaky!"

"It would be worse than freaky," I said. "It would be a nightmare."

We rode along the sidewalk and then turned a corner. We were almost to the college.

But farther down the street, several police cars came into view. Their lights were flashing and there were policemen all over the place, along with a fire truck and several other cars. From where we were, we couldn't see what had happened, but as we approached, we could definitely see that something was really wrong.

"Hey, look!" Stephen said. He skidded his bike to a stop. "What's that on the ground?"

We braked and stopped, and looked where Stephen was pointing.

"Oh my gosh!" Heather exclaimed. "Is that what I think it is?"

It was hard to see because there were so many police cars and people . . . but there was something laying across the road.

Something long and snake-like.

19

"Let's get closer," I said, and we rode on, slowly approaching the scene in front of us.

"I'll bet the giant anaconda got loose!" Stephen said.

But when we got closer and saw what it actually was, I started laughing.

"There's your giant anaconda," I said, slowing my bike to a stop. "A telephone pole!"

Sure enough, there was a telephone pole laying all the way across the street. We were close enough now to hear people talking and we found out that a truck had lost its brakes, gone out of control, and hit the telephone pole. Luckily, no one was injured in the accident.

"Some snake," Heather smirked.

We hopped off our bikes and pushed them alongside as we wound our way around the crowd. Then we jumped back on and began pedaling.

In a few minutes, we were winding our way through the college entrance. The college here isn't very big—certainly not like a college in Pittsburgh or Philadelphia—so it was easy to find the main office. Sure enough, Mr. Plumbody had left three visitor passes at the front desk for us.

The lady behind the counter gave us directions to get to Mr. Plumbody's laboratory.

"We're going to see his snakes," I told her, and she shuddered.

"Ewww," she said, cringing. "I hate snakes. They're all slimy and icky."

"No, they're not," Heather said. "They're not slimy at all."

"And they're not icky, either," Stephen added.

The lady shuddered again, then returned to doing paperwork.

We walked down the hall, made several turns, then finally came to a door with a big sign out front. I read it out loud.

"Herpetology," I said. "Mr. Plumbody, herpetologist."

"Looks like we got the right place," Stephen said.

Heather opened the door, and we stepped inside.

The room was small. There was a single desk with papers piled all over it. Pictures of snakes hung on the walls. There were papers on the floor, and even on the chair behind the desk. Mr. Plumbody was nowhere to be found.

"Mr. Plumbody is pretty messy," Heather whispered.

"Hey, he's a snake expert," I said. "Snake experts are supposed to be messy."

"They are?" Stephen asked.

"Yeah. At least, that's what I tell my mom."

On one wall was a picture of Mr. Plumbody. He was holding a very large, black snake. It was draped around his neck and over his shoulders.

83

"Look at the size of that thing!" I exclaimed, stepping toward the picture for a closer look.

"I wonder where Mr. Plumbody is," Heather said. "He said he was . . . *oh my gosh!*" she gasped. *"Ryan! Don't move! Don't move an inch!"*

I froze, and for a moment the only sound I could hear was the thump of my heart in my chest.

"Holy Toledo!" Stephen cried. "It's right at your feet!"

Without moving, I glanced down at the floor. A flood of terror nearly swept me away.

There, on the floor, only inches from my foot, was a rattlesnake.

A *big* rattlesnake.

It was coiled up, its tail in the air, head drawn back. Its mouth was open, and I could see inch-long fangs, sharp as needles, protruding down.

The snake was preparing to strike!

CHECKOUT RECEIPT
Mission Viejo Library
To renew or check acct status

Call (949) 855-8068
OR
Access your account online
at www.cmvl.org

User ID: M10350S429

Title: Pokémon shield [Nintendo
Switch]
Item ID: V000052731 61
Due: 6/29/2022,23:59

Total checkouts for session:1

Total checkouts:5

"When are my books due?"
Due by 11:59 PM
Check the status online
*
NEED A PASSPORT?
email passports@
cityofmissionviejo.org
or call (949) 470-8420

20

I stayed as still as I possibly could. There was no question that if the snake struck, I would be in serious trouble.

"You'd think he'd keep these things in cages!" I heard Stephen whisper fearfully.

"One must have got out," Heather replied. *"Stay as still as you can, Ryan . . . I'll go get help."*

I didn't say a word, and I didn't move. My eyes were riveted to the venomous viper that lay coiled at my feet.

Out of the corner of my eye, I saw Heather turn to walk out the door.

She didn't get far.

The door opened, and Mr. Plumbody came in.

"Well, hello there!" he said. "You children are right on time!"

"Mr. Plumbody!" Heather exclaimed. "It's Ryan! Look! We've got to do something!"

There was silence for a moment, then I could see more movement out of the corner of my eye.

"Well, well, what have we here?" Mr. Plumbody said as he walked toward me.

"Careful, Mr. Plumbody!" Stephen said. "That snake is pretty mad!"

"He is, is he?" Mr. Plumbody replied. And with that, he bent over and picked up the coiled snake.

I jumped back to a safe distance. A surge of relief flowed through me.

"No problem here," Mr. Plumbody explained. Then he carefully placed the coiled rattlesnake on his cluttered desk. "Stuffed, you see. Mounted. I found him dead on the side of the road when I was studying in Arizona. I took him to a taxidermist and had him mounted. Handsome creature, don't you think?"

"Stuffed!?!?" I gasped, taking a step toward the rattlesnake. "It sure looks real!"

"Well, he is real, sort of," Mr. Plumbody said. "But let's be on our way, and I'll show you some actual, real, *live* snakes," he said.

Wow! This was going to be too cool! We were going to get our own private tour of Mr. Plumbody's herpetology lab!

We followed him out of his office and down the hall, not knowing that what we were about to discover was only the beginning of our journey.

Our journey—into terror.

21

We walked down the hall, and Mr. Plumbody explained more about what he did at the college.

"I am a professor," he said, "and I am very involved in my study of snakes. I have the opportunity to study many different kinds of snakes from all over the world. I will show you a few of them this morning."

We went through a series of double doors and into a large room.

"This," Mr. Plumbody said proudly, "is my laboratory."

We just stared. The room looked nothing like a laboratory, at all.

I guess I expected the lab to be all white with bright lights . . . yet that's not the way it was at all.

There were wood counters along the walls and rows of wood tables. Lights hung from the ceiling, but they were a dull white . . . not at all the kind of bright, hospital-white that you might expect.

The floor was a gray tile, speckled with different colored stones.

And everywhere you looked, there were glass cases, each with a different kind of snake.

"Wow," I breathed, as my eyes darted around. On the far side of the room was a huge glass case with what appeared to be a huge tree branch inside. Mr. Plumbody saw me looking at it.

"Ah," he said, "you've found our largest snake. A boa constrictor, from South America. Come. Have a closer look."

We walked past a row of smaller cases and approached the large case. The boa constrictor was huge, and I recognized it right away.

"That's the snake that we saw a couple days ago!" I exclaimed.

Mr. Plumbody nodded. "That's right. It was able to escape by going through one of the air vents. We still haven't exactly figured out how it got out, but the custodians are looking into it. Hopefully, they'll fix the problem before any more mishaps occur."

Mr. Plumbody told us all about the boa constrictor, and then he showed us some different kinds of snakes. Some of the snakes were very poisonous. Others were nonpoisonous. Those he took out and let us hold. It was really cool.

"But the most poisonous snake of all," he said as he looked at us, "is a snake that no one knows about."

"What do you mean by that?" Heather asked.

"I mean that it was just discovered in the rain forest. It's an unknown species of a python that is so deadly, so poisonous, that we can't even keep them in the same room with the other snakes. This species of a snake was just discovered, and ten of them have been sent here for me to study. I'll be using the actual venom from these pythons to create an antidote."

"Poisonous pythons?!?!" Stephen exclaimed. "Like . . . how big are they?"

"Huge," Mr. Plumbody replied. "Some of them are bigger than the boa constrictor."

I looked around. "Well . . . where are they?" I asked.

"We keep them in a separate room. Would you like to see them?"

"Is it going to be safe?" Stephen asked.

"Perfectly," replied Mr. Plumbody. "Follow me."

We had no idea that our day was about to be turned upside down.

22

We followed Mr. Plumbody out of the laboratory and back down the hall. I could hardly contain my excitement. We were going to get to see a type of snake that no one else in the world has seen!

"The poisonous pythons," he explained, "are kept in another room with special, extra-thick glass. They are too dangerous to handle with bare hands. However, I have developed a special gas that, when sprayed in their face, causes the snake to fall asleep."

"Doesn't that hurt them?" Heather asked.

"Not at all," Mr. Plumbody said, shaking his head. "I would never want to harm these snakes."

"But how does the gas work?" I asked.

"It is dispensed from a tank that looks like a fire extinguisher. When the gas is sprayed into the snake's face, the snake breathes it in . . . causing it to fall asleep almost instantly. The snake usually remains asleep for almost an hour, until the effects of the gas wears off. Ah. Here we are."

We stopped at a large, white door. There was a sign above it that read *DANGER—ABSOLUTELY NO ADMITTANCE.*

Mr. Plumbody pulled some keys from his pocket. "We keep this locked at all times," he said. "These snakes are far too dangerous. I would hate to think what would happen to someone if they came into contact with these venomous creatures."

He unlocked the door and pushed it open. We followed him through. Directly in front of us was a large glass window. In fact, the entire wall was a window. On the other side of the glass was what appeared to be a jungle, filled with tree branches and leaves.

"We've tried to recreate the actual habitat that these snakes live in," Mr. Plumbody explained. "Come. Let's have a look."

We approached the large window. "They blend in really good," I said. "I can't even see any."

"Yes, they do," Mr. Plumbody said. But there was a sound in his voice that seemed different.

"Where are they?" Heather asked.

"They should be in there, somewhere," Mr. Plumbody said, and I could tell by his voice that he was nervous. His eyes were darting all over the place, scanning the inside of the enormous glass case.

"Something's wrong," he said. "Something is very wrong."

We all looked into the large case, but one thing was for sure: there were no snakes in it.

"There must be a reason for this," Mr. Plumbody said. "This just can't be!"

"What about that vent cover over there?" Stephen said, pointing to a corner in the case. "Is that supposed to be like that?"

When Mr. Plumbody saw the vent, his face went completely white. His eyes widened, and his jaw slackened.

"Oh no!" he said. "That's not supposed to be like that! That's not supposed to be like that at all!"

Now I was getting really worried. So was Heather.

"Like what?" she asked. "What's wrong?"

"The vent cover! It's broken! That means—"

What he said next caused icy tendrils of fear to slither through my body and wrap themselves around my heart.

"It means the snakes have escaped! Not only have they escaped . . . but they're outside, at this very moment!"

Ten of the most poisonous snakes in the world had gotten loose.

In a small town in Pennsylvania.

Our town.

In short . . . the city of Maple Glen was in for more trouble than it could imagine.

23

Talk about panic! Mr. Plumbody wasted no time, and sprang into action. He grabbed a tank that looked like a fire extinguisher.

"You must go home! Now!" he ordered. "Stay on the sidewalk, and don't go into the woods or the swamp!"

"But where are the snakes?" I asked.

"I don't know," Mr. Plumbody said. "But I've got to find them. Now go! Go home and stay there!" Then he hurried out the door carrying the large spray cannister.

"Let's get out of here!" Stephen exclaimed. "I don't want to be hanging around and get bitten by a giant poisonous snake!"

We ran out of the room and down the hall. Soon, we were outside, leaping onto our bikes. I looked over and saw two college students. They were sitting on the grass, chatting.

"Get inside!" I told one of them. "The poisonous pythons are loose!"

They looked over at me like I was crazy, then resumed their conversation.

"No, really!" I said. "There's a bunch of poisonous pythons loose!"

This time they ignored me all together.

"Come on!" Heather said. "You heard what Mr. Plumbody said! Let's get out of here!"

We sped away on our bikes, but I couldn't help looking into the woods, wondering if I would catch a glimpse of one of the pythons. Every time I saw a branch that twisted and turned, I looked twice to see if it was a snake.

A police siren sounded, and we could hear it drawing near. Then it appeared ahead of us on the road. In a few seconds it whirred past, on its way to the college.

"Man, I bet everybody in the city is going to freak out when they find out about the snakes!" Stephen said.

We passed the spot at the park where we usually locked up our bikes before going into the swamp.

Suddenly, Heather skidded her bike to a halt. I slowed and looked back over my shoulder, but I didn't stop.

"What?!?!" I shouted back to her. "What is it?!?!"

"I heard someone shouting for help!" Heather said. "Listen!"

I braked to a halt, turned around, and pedaled back to where Heather was. Stephen joined us.

"Listen," she said. "It sounded like someone was calling for help!"

We were silent for a moment. The park was empty, and the only sounds I could hear were the sounds of cars in the distance and a few birds chirping in some trees nearby.

"I think you're hearing things," I said. "I don't hear anything."

"I know what I heard," Heather said. "It sounded like someone calling out for help."

We listened some more, but didn't hear anything.

"Come on," Stephen said. "It was probably just the wind in the trees."

Stephen started pedaling off. Just then, I heard a cry from the swamp. It was a long way off, but there was no doubt about it . . . someone was shouting for help!

"Stephen! Wait!" I shouted, and he turned back around again and stopped. "There *is* someone in the swamp!" I exclaimed.

"Huh-uh, no way, no how," Stephen said, shaking his head. "I know what you're thinking. No way."

I looked at Heather, and she looked at me. Then we heard another shout from the swamp.

"We've got to help him," she said, getting off her bike. I joined her.

"No way," Stephen shouted. "I'm not going into the swamp. Not with those poisonous pythons loose!"

"Stephen, we've got to help. Someone is in trouble. They might not even know the danger they're in."

He stopped his bike, but I could tell he didn't want to go into the swamp.

"We'll be all right," I said, "as long as we stick together."

Stephen shook his head, but he reluctantly got off his bike and starting running toward us.

"This isn't a good idea," he said.

"Good idea or not, someone needs help," Heather said.

And I agreed. I didn't think it was a good idea to go into the swamp with those poisonous pythons on the loose, but I told myself that the snakes were probably somewhere else. After all, even if they were in there, the swamp was so big that we probably wouldn't even run across a python.

I was wrong.

24

We heard the voice shout for help again.

"Hey!" I shouted. "Can you hear us?!?!"

We waited for a moment, but didn't hear a reply.

"Maybe he's lost," Heather said.

"Or maybe he got bit by a poisonous python," Stephen said.

"You always think the worst, don't you?" I said to him.

"Hey, we don't know. Maybe he's being attacked by a python right now."

"Come on," Heather said. "He's probably just lost. Let's go find him and lead him out."

So we entered the swamp.

The sun was starting to sink in the west. The evening was warm. As we pushed the thick branches out of our way, mosquitos buzzed around our heads. I stepped in a soft spot and mud went up over my ankles.

"Help!" we heard again.

"We're coming!" I shouted.

We continued through the swamp in the direction of the voice.

But I must say . . . I was a little nervous, knowing that those pythons had escaped.

They're a long way away, I told myself. *Besides . . . Mr. Plumbody has probably already caught them and returned them to their cage.*

We walked and walked, but the going was slow. The swamp was so thick and the branches were so dense that we had to push them out of our way before we took a step.

"I've never been this deep in the swamp," Stephen said.

"Neither have I," I replied.

We could still hear the kid shouting for help. Finally, after Heather called out to him, he answered.

"Over here!" he shouted. "I'm over here!"

"That way," I said, pointing in the direction of the voice. "He's over there."

"Stay where you are!" Heather shouted. "We'll find you!"

We pressed on. After a moment, I heard brush snapping. Through the branches, I could see a flash of blue and white.

"There he is!" Stephen said.

It was a boy, a little younger than I. He was all dirty from scrambling through the swamp.

"You found me!" he said.

"How did you get here?" Stephen asked.

"I walked here," the boy replied.

"No," Heather said. "Why are you here, so deep in the swamp?"

"I was chasing a frog," the boy said. "He was a big one. I couldn't let him get away. I guess I got lost."

"Well, we found you," I said. "But we have to get out of here. There's a bunch of poisonous snakes that have escaped from the college."

When I said this, I thought he was going to cry.

"Hey, don't worry," Heather said. "You're safe with us. What's your name?"

"Jake," the boy said.

"Well, come on, Jake. Let's go home."

"I think we go this way," Stephen said.

"No," I replied. "We go this way over here."

"Are you sure?" Heather said.

I looked around. The swamp was so dense, so thick, that every direction looked the same.

"I'm pretty sure," I said. "But ... well ... not really."

At that moment, we realized something. We had hiked into the swamp to help a lost boy.

Now we were lost ourselves.

"Okay," I said. "We have to stay calm. We'll find our way out of here."

"I'm not worried about finding our way out of here," Stephen said. "I'm worried about those poisonous pythons finding us."

"They aren't going to find us," I said. "They're probably not anywhere even close."

But when we heard the branches cracking and snapping close by, I knew that I was wrong.

We were about to have our first encounter with a snake.

Not just *any* snake, either.

A poisonous python.

25

"What was that?" Jake whispered.

"Probably nothing," I said.

But I wasn't so sure.

Branches continued to snap, and I could hear a light crunching on the ground.

"Nobody move," I said quietly. "Stay as still as you can."

We remained frozen. I held my breath. The sound was getting closer.

Then I caught a movement, and I saw something brown moving slowly.

And it looked like—

It was! It was a snake! And it was huge!

There was no doubt about it . . . it had to be one of the poisonous pythons that had escaped from the college!

The snake wasn't *really* big . . . but it was big enough. It was as big around as a baseball bat, and it was colored with splotches of brown, green, black and beige.

I could see Stephen tremble. I was shaking, too. If that snake saw us . . . .

Seconds passed, and the snake kept moving. It was only a few feet away, but so far, it hadn't spotted us.

Just a few more minutes, I thought. *Just a few more minutes and it'll be gone.*

Time moved like a turtle. The snake seemed to be in no hurry, and it slithered along slow and steady. Every few moments it would stop, turn its head, and flick out its long, forked tongue.

Soon, the snake was out of sight. We waited for what seemed like a long time, just to be sure that the serpent wouldn't hear us and come back.

"We've got to get out of here," Heather said.

"I'm all for that," Stephen said.

"I want to go home," Jake said.

"Guys, we have two big problems," I said. "First of all, we're lost. Second of all, if we *do* try and make it out of the swamp, we risk running into one of those things again." I pointed in the direction that the snake had gone. "And I have a bad feeling that the snake we saw was probably one of the smaller ones."

"Well, then, what do we do?" Stephen said.

"We wait," I replied. "We wait right here. Sooner or later, people will come looking for us. Someone is bound to realize that we're gone, and they'll find us."

"Man, my mom and dad are going to be steamed if they have to come out here in the swamp to find me."

"I don't care who finds us," Heather said. "I don't want to share this swamp with gigantic, deadly snakes."

"Well, I think the best thing to do is wait. Everybody agree?"

"Okay," Stephen said.

"Yeah," Heather replied.

"I want to go home," Jake said.

"You'll get home, Jake, but we'll have to wait for help. All right?"

"Okay," he said.

So that's what we did. We waited. And we waited some more.

Soon, the sunlight started fading. The sky went from blue to orange, then to yellow, then to pink.

It grew darker.

No one came.

Darkness swept over the swamp, and it was difficult to see.

We didn't speak to each other very much, but we all knew what we were about to face.

Nighttime in the swamp.

Just the four of us.

Nighttime in the swamp . . . with deadly poisonous pythons slithering all around us!

26

Darkness.

Stars blinked from the black heavens above. The moon crept up, providing at least a little bit of light for us to see . . . but not much.

And the sounds! We heard crickets and owls and tree frogs. The day creatures had gone to bed, and the night creatures were out to play.

We huddled together. One good thing: the temperature hadn't gone down much. Sometimes in Pennsylvania, even in the summer, the nights can get chilly. So far, it was still pretty warm, so none of us got cold.

"It won't be much longer now," I said hopefully. Actually, I wasn't really sure, but my dad always says that it's best to look on the positive side of things.

"You're right," Heather replied. "I'll bet our parents are looking for us right now."

"I'll bet they're not," Stephen said sorrowfully.

"What are you talking about?" I asked. "Of course they are. They know that we're missing and they're looking for us right now. I'm sure they've found our bikes by the park, and any minute someone will find us."

In the glow of the moonlight, I saw Stephen shake his head. "Nope," he said. "I'll bet that word is out about the escaped poisonous pythons. I'll bet they know that the snakes are in the swamp, and they're not going to let anyone go into the swamp until all the snakes are caught."

My heart hit the ground.

Stephen is right, I thought. *I'll bet they have a hundred police cars blocking off the swamp. There's no way they're going to let anyone in the swamp until they find those snakes. It would be too dangerous.*

"Well, either way," Heather said, "they'll find us. We might have to wait until morning, but they'll find us."

Jake started to sniffle, and I thought he was going to cry. I put my arm over his shoulders.

"Hey, buddy," I said. "Don't worry. We're going to make it out of here. Don't be afraid."

"I guess . . . I guess this is all my fault," he stammered, and he sniffled again. "I was the one who was lost, and you guys were just trying to help. If it hadn't been for me, you guys would already be home."

I could tell he felt really bad.

"It's not your fault," Heather said. "It's nobody's fault. I wouldn't—"

Suddenly, Heather stopped talking.

"What?" Stephen said. "What is it?"

"Did you hear that?" Heather said.

We all listened.

"There it is!" she hissed. "It's a helicopter! I'm sure of it!"

Heather was right! We could hear the whirring *thumpthumpthump* of helicopter blades chopping through the night sky. Very soon, it was really loud, and then—

"Look!" Stephen shouted. "There it is!"

To the south, we could see the blinking lights of the helicopter as it approached. It was beaming down a huge ray of light—a searchlight. The bright shaft of light cut the night like a sword.

"We're rescued!" Jake said. "They've found us!"

"Not yet, they haven't," I said. "Quick! Everybody wave their arms and yell!"

And that's exactly what we did. We screamed our lungs out and waved our arms wildly, and jumped up and down.

But as the helicopter drew near, it was obvious that they hadn't spotted us . . . and they weren't going to. The chopper turned and began to search in another direction.

No one said a thing as the blinking lights of the helicopter disappeared from sight. The sound of the motor slowly faded until it was quiet once again.

Now, the only sounds were those of the creatures in the swamp. Crickets, frogs; an occasional hoot of an owl. Mosquitos buzzing by our ears.

And one thing more.

A slow, soft, crunching sound.

The sound of branches being moved.

Something wasn't far away.

And it was coming closer and closer with each passing second.

27

Terror settled over us like a thick blanket, dark and suffocating. We stood there motionless, listening to the sound of crunching and the snapping of twigs.

"It's getting closer," Heather whispered. *"It's coming right toward us!"*

"I'll bet it heard us," Stephen said. *"I'll bet it heard us making all that racket when the helicopter came. We probably made it mad."*

Whatever was making the sound was only a few feet away.

"Okay guys," I whispered. *"Remember: stay perfectly still, just like last time."*

"You don't have to tell me," Stephen muttered.

The sound was so close that it drove me nuts! Whatever it was, it had to be right at our feet. I was afraid to look down for fear of moving.

"Oh, it's cute!" Heather suddenly exclaimed.

What?!?!? I thought. *How can a poisonous python be cute?!?!*

I looked down.

Right at my feet was a raccoon! It was about the size of a house cat, and it was just wandering by without a care in the world.

Boy, what a relief! Still, I didn't move. I didn't want to scare the critter. Raccoons are cute, but it's best to just leave them alone.

After a few moments, the raccoon was gone. I started to giggle, and then Heather did, too. Soon, we were all laughing at the fact that we'd allowed ourselves to become terrified. . . by an ordinary little raccoon!

The only thing we could do was wait, and that's exactly what we did. When we talked to one another, we kept our voices to a soft whisper. Mostly, we talked about the trouble we would get in when we were found.

And we heard the helicopter a few more times, too, but it didn't come very close. Finally, it dawned on us that we probably would be spending the entire night in the swamp.

Until we heard another sound.

A voice!

We could hear a voice in the distance, and there was no mistaking who it was.

Mr. Plumbody!

He was calling our names!

We all began shouting at once.

"Shhh!" I said. "We have to listen to see if he's heard us!"

We listened, and, sure enough, we heard his voice again, faint, but clear.

"Are you all right?!?!"

"Yes!" I shouted back. "But we're lost!"

"Stay right where you are," he shouted again, *"and I'll come to you. Just keep talking to me every few seconds so I can follow your voice!"*

We did just as he said, and I can't tell you how happy I was when I could see broken pieces of light filtering through the swamp.

Rescued! Mr. Plumbody had found us! We were going to go home! The nightmare had finally come to end . . . .

But not *quite.*

Because as Mr. Plumbody got closer, we realized that something else was coming closer, too . . . and in the light of the moon, we suddenly saw the most horrifying sight I could have ever imagined.

A python.

It was nestled on a branch in a nearby tree. It slithered part way down the branch and then opened its mouth wide. Its long, sharp fangs glowed in the moonlight. It hissed, and its forked tongue licked at the night air.

That's when we realized that our night of terror was only beginning.

28

We didn't dare breathe, much less move. The snake was so close that there was no way we would be able to get away if we tried to run.

If the snake wanted to attack, it would.

Beyond the deadly snake, we could see the flicker of Mr. Plumbody's light coming closer and closer.

"Where are you?" he called out.

"Right . . . right . . . here," I managed to stammer. "But . . . but . . . there's a snake . . . a snake here, too."

Mr. Plumbody stopped moving. The beam of light swept toward us, illuminating the snake.

"Okay," Mr. Plumbody said. "Listen carefully. Don't make a move. Not one inch."

Yeah . . . like that was going to be a problem! We were so scared, we couldn't have moved if we tried. In the beam of Mr. Plumbody's flashlight, the snake looked more menacing than ever.

Mr. Plumbody began walking again. I could hear him pushing branches out of his way, stepping over bushes, and snapping twigs.

Sensing another intruder, the snake suddenly turned away from us. It was still hanging from the tree branch, but at any moment it could slither down, or strike at us . . . or both.

"Okay," Mr. Plumbody said. "On the count of three, I want all of you to fall to the ground and cover your faces. Got it?"

"Okay," I answered.

"Good." Mr. Plumbody took another few steps closer . . . and this made the snake mad. It struck out, aiming for him, but Mr. Plumbody ducked aside.

"Okay," he said. "One . . . two . . . *three!*"

We fell to the ground and did exactly what he asked. I sure hoped he knew what he was doing!

I heard a hissing sound, but it didn't sound like the snake. This was another type of hiss all together, like a blast of air escaping from a balloon.

"Ha! Gotcha!" I heard Mr. Plumbody exclaim. "Are you guys okay?"

"Yeah," Heather answered.

"Good. Stay where you are for another moment."

A minute went by, and then we heard Mr. Plumbody moving.

"Okay," he said. "It's safe now."

We scrambled to our feet and turned to Mr. Plumbody. Hanging from the tree was the python . . . fast asleep!

"That was a close one," Stephen said. "That thing almost got us!"

"You are all very lucky," Mr. Plumbody said, and he explained what had been going on the past few hours. He said that he and Mr. Larson, along with some lab assistants, had been rounding up the snakes all day, and that they'd caught most of them. He also said that everyone in Maple Glen was ordered to stay in their homes until all of the snakes had been captured.

"But what about our parents?" Heather asked.

"Oh, your parents sure are worried," he said. Then he reached down to his waist and plucked up his cell phone. "I'll call the police right now and let them know you're all right."

Well, that was another relief. At least our moms and dads would know that we were okay.

He spoke for a few minutes, and then he put the phone away.

"All right, guys," he said. "Let's go home."

For a moment, I felt like cheering.

For a moment.

Soon, I wouldn't feel like cheering at all.

Soon, I would be screaming.

29

I was wondering just how we were going to get out of the forest without getting lost.

I shouldn't have worried. Mr. Plumbody had a compass, and he pulled it out and shined his light on it.

"We go this way," he said. "Everybody stick together and stay close."

I was so glad to be on our way home. The thought of spending the rest of the night in the swamp with those pythons freaked me out.

"We found out how the pythons escaped," Mr. Plumbody explained as we trudged through the thick swamp. "The air vent cover was loose. One of the smaller snakes was probably able to wriggle out, pushing the vent cover off. This allowed the rest of the snakes to escape, too. We've already fixed it so that it will never happen again."

Every few minutes Mr. Plumbody would stop and consult his compass to make sure we were still headed the right direction. I decided that the next time I ever headed out into the woods or swamp, I would make sure that I had one of those. If we'd had a compass with us earlier, we would have never gotten lost.

We walked for a long time. It seemed like it took a lot longer getting out of the swamp than it did coming in.

"We shouldn't be far now," Mr. Plumbody said. "Everybody doing okay?"

"Yeah," I said.

"I'm fine," Heather replied.

"I'm getting tired," said Stephen.

"Yeah, me too," echoed Jake.

"Well, we only have a little bit farther to go," Mr. Plumbody said.

Which was true—but we didn't count on what happened next.

Mr. Plumbody had stopped to check his compass. All of a sudden, we heard a terrible hiss. The light Mr. Plumbody was carrying fell to the ground. We heard him cry out.

There was no doubt as to what had happened.

Mr. Plumbody had been attacked by a poisonous python.

30

We could hear Mr. Plumbody struggling, but the flashlight had fallen to the ground. The beam was pointing off in a different direction. Mr. Plumbody was gasping and trying to say something, but we couldn't tell what it was.

Heather was closest to the flashlight, so she leaped forward and grabbed it. When she swept the beam at Mr. Plumbody, we all screamed.

What we saw was horrifying.

An enormous python had wrapped itself around Mr. Plumbody! He was on the ground, and his arms were pinned to his sides by the giant snake. He couldn't move! The large cannister of spray that he had been using to sedate the snakes was on the ground. The snake hadn't bitten him, but I knew that it was only a matter of seconds before it did.

There was only one thing I could do, and I did it without even thinking about it. I dove forward, reaching for the spray cannister . . . but I tripped, and landed right on top of the snake and Mr. Plumbody!

The snake hissed at me, but quickly returned its attention to Mr. Plumbody.

I rolled to the side, grabbed the cannister, and stood up. I aimed the spray at the python's head, and pushed down on the lever.

A fine mist shot out of the nozzle, engulfing the snake and Mr. Plumbody. The snake turned its head and looked right at me. It opened its mouth to strike. But the spray had already done its work. The snake teetered to one side, then another. It was having a hard time holding its head up.

Then, its head simply went limp and it fell to the ground.

The snake was asleep!

"Mr. Plumbody!" I shouted. "Get away from it! It's asleep!"

But Mr. Plumbody didn't move.

"Come on!" I shouted. "We've got to get him away from the snake!"

Heather was still holding the flashlight, and she drew close.

The snake was still wrapped around Mr. Plumbody, so I started to pull it away from him. Stephen jumped in to help, and so did Jake. It took a lot of work, but we were finally able to get Mr. Plumbody free.

But he wasn't moving!

"Mr. Plumbody! Can you hear me?!?!" I shouted.

But it was no use. The snake had done its work, and we were sure that Mr. Plumbody was dead.

31

"Is . . . is he . . . is he dead?" Jake stammered.

I dropped to my knees and placed my ear to his chest.

"I can hear his heart beating! He's alive!"

Suddenly, Mr. Plumbody made a sound.

He was snoring!

"He's . . . he's only asleep!" Heather said. "He's not dead at all!"

Then I realized what had happened. When I had sprayed the snake, Mr. Plumbody must have breathed in some of the mist, causing him to fall asleep, too.

"Help me try and wake him up!" I said.

We tried everything we could to wake him, but it was no use.

"Hey," Stephen said. "Let's just use his cell phone and call for help."

"Great idea!" I said.

The cell phone was still clipped to Mr. Plumbody's waist, but when I picked it up, it was obvious we wouldn't be using *this* phone to call anybody.

The phone was crushed.

"The snake must have broken it when it was wrapped around him," I said.

"Now what?" Heather asked.

"We do exactly what we did a couple of hours ago," I said.

"What's that?" Stephen asked.

"We yell for help. Maybe we're close enough to the edge of the swamp that someone will hear us."

So that's what we did. We screamed our heads off, calling for help, but nobody came. We didn't hear or see the helicopter, either.

All of a sudden, I saw something shiny on the ground.

The compass!

I snapped it up and looked at it, then my spirits went into a tailspin.

The compass was broken, too!

So, we were stuck once again. We were still in the forest, lost, not knowing where to go. And we couldn't just leave Mr. Plumbody here!

And now we had another problem.

The huge python was still on the ground, fast asleep.

But not for long.

The snake's tail began to twitch! It was waking up!

32

We watched in horror as the python's tail began to move, and I knew it was only going to be a matter of minutes before the python woke up.

But Mr. Plumbody was still sleeping!

"Can't we just spray the snake again?" Heather asked.

"Yeah, we could," I replied. "But we still need to get Mr. Plumbody away from the python. Come on. Let's see if we can move him."

Heather put the light down, aiming the beam toward Mr. Plumbody. The four of us grabbed him by the ankles and began to pull.

"Geez, he weighs a ton!" Stephen said.

"It would be a lot easier moving him if we weren't in the swamp," I said.

We struggled and struggled. Slowly, we were able to drag him away from the python. All the while, Mr. Plumbody snored away, sleeping peacefully.

"There," I said. "That should be far enough. Now, if we need to spray the snake again, we won't accidentally spray Mr. Plumbody."

And it was a good thing we moved him, too, because the snake was moving faster now. Its whole body began to twitch. I knew it was waking up.

I picked up the spray cannister and waited. The snake raised its head, real groggy-like, but I wasn't going to give it a chance. I gave it another blast of spray. The snake sunk back into a stupor, and soon it was asleep again.

And that's when our luck finally began to change . . . for the better.

I had just finished spraying the snake, when I heard a noise.

"It's the helicopter!" Stephen shouted. *"Look! It's over there!"*

"Heather! Quick! Grab the light and shine it up in the air! Shine it at the helicopter to let them know where we are!"

Heather didn't waste any time. She picked up the flashlight and aimed the beam into the night sky. Soon, the helicopter came into view. She aimed the beam of light directly at it, and, just for good measure, she blinked it a few times.

It worked! The pilot saw the light, and the helicopter turned and headed toward us!

Then, a searchlight appeared, and we were suddenly standing in light as bright as day. The helicopter hovered right above us, unmoving, keeping the searchlight trained on us.

The roar of the whirring blades was deafening, and the churning wind tossed branches and leaves all over. It was like being in a hurricane. Heather's hair blew all over the place, and she gathered it up and held onto it with her hands.

"What's he doing?!?!" Stephen shouted over the deafening roar of the chopper.

"I think he's showing the other searchers where we are!" I shouted back. "By hovering over us with the light, he's leading other people to where we are!"

And that's exactly what happened. Very soon, we could see another light coming toward us.

Soon, there were people surrounding us, including Mr. Larson, the pet store owner! One of the men was carrying a large bag, and the other had a powerful flashlight.

"You don't know how glad we are to see you!" I shouted.

"You're fine, now," Mr. Larson said.

The two other men knelt down next to Mr. Plumbody.

"I think he's okay," I said. "I had to use the spray to keep the snake from attacking him. He breathed in some of the spray and fell asleep."

One of the men removed a small item from his pocket, and he waved it beneath Mr. Plumbody's nose.

Instantly, Mr. Plumbody came to. He shook his head and blinked his eyes a few times.

"Wow, what was that?" I asked Mr. Larson.

"Smelling salts," Mr. Larson replied. "It's a very strong odor, and it's used to wake people up after they have fainted."

The helicopter rose up into the sky, but the searchlight remained trained on us. The two other men helped Mr. Plumbody to his feet, holding onto his arms to help him keep his balance. He looked a little confused, like he didn't know where he was or how he'd gotten there. After a few moments, he was his normal self again.

The snake was still asleep, and we watched as the two men, along with Mr. Larson, and Mr. Plumbody, struggled to put it in a large leather bag. Because the snake was so big and heavy, it took them a few minutes. Finally, they succeeded. The snake was so heavy that it took two men to carry the bag.

"We're not far from the college," Mr. Larson said. "Come on. We'll all stick together and hike out."

At last . . . our python nightmare had ended. Almost.

Because Mr. Larson didn't tell us that there was still one python that they hadn't caught yet.

It was the oldest and the biggest python of the bunch.

It was still loose, somewhere in the swamp.

And we were about to find it.

33

Mr. Plumbody and Mr. Larson were in front of us, and the two men carrying the bag were behind us. I sure was glad that we were on our way out of the swamp, but I also was worried about the trouble we would be in. I figured I'd probably get grounded for life.

But it could have been worse. One of us could have been bitten by one of the poisonous pythons . . . and that would have been a lot bigger problem than getting grounded.

Mr. Plumbody and Mr. Larson were talking to each other, but I couldn't hear what they were saying. The two men behind us grunted every once in a while as they struggled with the heavy bag that contained the poisonous python.

"Look up ahead!" Stephen said.

Lights! I could see the lights of the college through the thick branches.

And flashing red and blue police lights, too. I was sure they'd been very busy over the last few hours.

"We made it!" Heather cried. "We're almost home!"

The swamp began to thin, and it was easier walking. The thick, vine-like saplings gave way to bigger trees, and it wasn't near as difficult to move.

And suddenly—

Mr. Plumbody and Mr. Larson leaped backward, almost knocking me over.

"Back!" Mr. Plumbody shouted. *"Everybody back!"*

I scrambled backwards and bumped into Heather, who bumped into Stephen, who knocked Jake over. Jake leaped to his feet and backed up, and we huddled together, and peered into the murky forest ahead of us.

What I saw made me gasp.

A python.

He was gigantic! The snake was hanging from a tree branch, facing us. Its mouth was open, displaying razor-sharp fangs. The beam from Mr. Larson's flashlight glowed in the snake's eyes, making it look even more menacing.

And when I say it was *big*, I mean it was *BIG*. The python's head was as big as a basketball! I have never seen a snake so big in my life. Not even in pictures!

Mr. Plumbody sprang into action. He held up the spray cannister and aimed the nozzle at the snake's head.

"I'm too far away," he said, and he took a step closer. The snake swung back slowly, hissing angrily.

Mr. Plumbody took another step. I couldn't believe how close he was getting to the snake. If he didn't get close enough though, when he sprayed the mist, the snake would be able to dart out of the way.

"There," Mr. Plumbody said. "Close enough."

He pressed down on the top of the cannister—

But nothing happened!

He pressed again, harder this time. Still, nothing happened.

"It's empty!" he shouted. "Get me another cannister! Quick!"

Mr. Larson was already reaching out with his cannister . . . but it was too late. The snake reared back, opened its mouth wide, and struck. There was no way Mr. Plumbody would be able to move fast enough to escape.

34

Mr. Plumbody wouldn't be able to move fast enough, and he knew it.

So, he did the only thing he could do.

He grasped the spray cannister with both hands, turned it sideways, and held it up in the air to block the attacking snake.

The python's jaws clamped around the cannister, and Mr. Plumbody let go. The snake drew back, the silver cannister in its mouth. I could see venom dripping from its fangs. I was horrified to think of what might have happened if

Mr. Plumbody . . . or any of us . . . would have been bitten.

Mr. Larson threw his spray cannister to Mr. Plumbody, who immediately turned toward the snake. The python dropped the cannister it had in its mouth, and prepared to strike again.

Mr. Plumbody, however, was ready this time. He aimed the nozzle at the snake and sprayed a thick, white mist at the snake's head. The python hissed and drew back, but it was too late. The mist had done its work, and the snake began to weave lazily back and forth. Then it slunk out of the tree and slid to the ground.

"It's getting away!" I shouted.

"No, it's not," Mr. Plumbody replied. "It's trying, but it won't. In a moment, it'll be fast asleep."

Mr. Plumbody was right. Soon, the snake had stopped moving. We waited for a moment to make sure, but the python never even flinched. It was asleep.

"That was a close one," Mr. Larson said.

"You're not kidding," Mr. Plumbody replied. "It's a good thing you had that cannister. Go on ahead and take these children up to the college. Bring back some more helpers, too. It's going to take a few more hands to carry *this* snake out of the woods."

We followed Mr. Larson out of the woods, and, sure enough, I spotted my parents waiting for me. Bright lights lit up the entire parking lot. There were police cars everywhere. Heather's mom and dad were there, along with Stephen's parents. I was sure that Jake's mom and dad were waiting, but I didn't see them.

And one thing was for certain:

I sure was glad to be out of the swamp. We had been really lucky, and none of us had been hurt. As it turned out, I didn't get into a lot of trouble, either. I didn't even get grounded! Mom and Dad said they were proud of me for coming to Jake's rescue when he had called for help, but they said next time to get an adult instead of trying to go that far into the swamp.

And as I crawled into bed that night, I felt so relieved that everything had turned out okay. I closed my eyes and fell asleep . . . not knowing

that, in the morning, the horror was about to
begin all over again.

35

When I woke up the next morning, I called Stephen to see what kind of trouble he was in. He said that his mom and dad had been pretty cool about the whole thing, and he wasn't grounded. He said he'd also talked to Heather earlier in the morning, and she wasn't grounded, but her parents had told her to never, ever go into the swamp again.

"I'm sure glad they caught all of those pythons," I said.

"Didn't you hear?" Stephen said. "It was on the news this morning. They think that there is still one poisonous python missing."

"No way!"

"Yep. That's what I heard. They don't know where it is, and they want everybody to keep an eye out for it."

"Well, you can bet I'm not going to go anywhere near it," I said.

"Me neither," Stephen replied. "Hey, I've got an idea. Hop on your bike and ride over here, and we'll go fishing down by the creek. I heard that somebody caught a big catfish there the other day."

That sounded like fun. I'd had enough snake-catching for a few days, and fishing down at the creek would be cool.

Besides . . . the creek was nowhere near the swamp. I wanted to stay far away from that place . . . at least until they caught that last python.

I ate a quick breakfast, then I gathered up my fishing pole from the garage.

But when I opened the garage door and pushed my bicycle out, I froze.

Fear hit me like a semi truck, and I couldn't move. I didn't dare.

Right in front of me, in the driveway, was a python!

36

I gasped, then held my breath. I didn't dare move a muscle. The python didn't move, either. He just lay there in the driveway in the morning sun, glaring up at me with wicked, sinister eyes.

After a moment, I heard giggling coming from the bushes at the side of our house.

Still, the snake didn't move.

I heard more giggling, and I recognized who it was.

Then I looked down at the snake.

"All right," I said with a laugh. "You got me!"

Suddenly, Stephen emerged from the bushes.

"Isn't that cool?!?!" he exclaimed as he walked toward me.

"It sure looks real!" I exclaimed.

"That's the one I showed you in that catalog," he explained. "It came in the mail yesterday. Man! We're going to have a lot of fun freaking people out with that! Just wait until school starts up again!"

He bent down and gathered up the rubber snake. Then he looped it around his neck. It sure looked like a real snake!

"So, there really isn't another poisonous python loose, is there?" I asked.

Stephen shook his head. "Nah," he said. "I just said that to set up the joke. After I hung up the phone, I ran over here and put the snake in front of your garage. Then I hid in the bushes and waited for you to come out."

I shook my head and smiled. After all, it was pretty funny. He really had me fooled for a minute.

I rode my bike slowly, as he walked along beside me. When we got to his house, Stephen put the snake in his room. Then he grabbed his fishing pole and hopped on his bike, and we rode across town to the creek.

We rode along a trail to a place where not many people know about: a small bend in the creek where there is a deep hole. The fishing there is usually pretty good.

When we got there, we were surprised to see that there was someone else already there. It was a girl, and she looked to be around our age. She was sitting on the bank, holding a fishing pole.

"I didn't think anybody else knew about this spot," I whispered.

"Neither did I," Stephen replied.

"Hi," I called out, and the girl jumped. She hadn't seen us, and we surprised her.

"Sorry about that," I said.

"It's okay," she said.

"Are you catching anything?" Stephen asked.

She shook her head. "No. I haven't caught a thing."

We walked up beside her.

"I'm Ryan," I said. "This is my friend, Stephen."

"I'm Serena," the girl said.

"Do you live here in Maple Glen?" I asked.

She shook her head. "No, I live in Delaware. I'm just visiting my grandparents who live here."

We talked to her for a few minutes, and then Stephen asked her if she'd heard about the poisonous pythons that had escaped yesterday.

"Yeah, I heard about it," she said. "We stayed inside until all of the snakes were caught."

We told her all about what had happened to us, and she said it sounded like a pretty scary ordeal.

"But not as scary as what happened to me in Delaware," she said.

"Why?" I asked. "What happened to you in Delaware?"

"It's kind of spooky," she said. "But it's true. It really happened to me and my brother."

"Like . . . how spooky?" Stephen asked.

"*Really* spooky," Serena said. "In fact, you probably wouldn't believe it if I told you. In fact, it's about dolls, so you probably wouldn't be interested."

"Dolls?!?!" I said. "How can dolls be scary?"

"Believe me . . . you would be afraid of *these* dolls," she said with a nod.

"Tell us what happened!" I said.

"Yeah!" Stephen echoed.

"Okay," she said. "But don't say I didn't warn you."

We sat down next to Serena and listened while she told us the spookiest story we had ever heard . . . .

NEXT IN THE THRILLING

AMERICAN CHILLERS

SERIES:

#12:

DANGEROUS

DOLLS

OF

DELAWARE

turn the page to read a few
spine-tingling chapters!

1

"Find anything?" I asked as I plunged the shovel into the dirt. My brother, Spencer, was kneeling on the ground near my feet, his hands sifting through the dark, wet ground.

"Nothing yet," he said. "But I'm sure we will. Try digging deeper, Serena."

That's me. Serena Boardman. I'm twelve, and my brother, Spencer, is eleven. He was planning on going fishing in a few hours, and I was helping him dig for worms in the woods not far from our house.

And so far, we hadn't had much luck . . . but that was about to change.

Only, it wasn't worms that we would be finding.

Not today.

I'd already dug a good-sized hole. Now, I stood over it and plunged the shovel blade into the ground again, digging the hole deeper.

There was a dull thud, and the shovel stopped abruptly.

"Uh oh," I said. "We're not going any deeper here. I think I hit a root."

I pulled the shovel out of the hole. Spencer reached down, grabbed a handful of dirt with his hand, and pulled it out.

Then he stopped.

"Hey," he said, peering down into the hole. "That doesn't look like a root. Check it out."

I dropped the shovel and knelt down. Spencer and I dug with our hands, clumping the dirt next to us in a growing pile.

"You're right!" I exclaimed. "This isn't a root at all!"

And it wasn't. Whatever was in the ground was made of wood, but it was too smooth and flat to be a root.

Birds chirruped from the trees. The air was cool and damp, and the gray sky hinted of a coming rainstorm.

"Keep digging around the sides," Spencer said. "I think it's some kind of box."

"Like a treasure chest!" I said.

"Yeah!" Spencer shouted. "Maybe it's a chest full of buried treasure!"

That would be cool!

"What's a box doing way out here in the woods, buried in the ground?" I asked, pulling out another clump of dark dirt. My hands were almost black from the clammy earth.

"You got me," Spencer replied. He reached down, grabbed a corner of the box, and pulled. The box moved a tiny bit.

I reached down and grabbed the other side of the box.

"On three," I said. "One, two, three!"

We lifted, and the wooden box came up. It wasn't really heavy, but it sure looked old. There was no doubt that it had been in the ground for a long, long time.

"It feels empty," Spencer said as we placed the box on the ground.

"So much for buried treasure," I said.

There wasn't any handles on the box, and the lid was nailed shut.

"I think I can get the blade of the shovel between the lid and the box," Spencer said, reaching for the shovel. "Then we can pry it off."

He wedged the metal blade into the thin crack and pumped the shovel up and down. The nails gave way easily, and the lid lifted.

And inside the box —

Two dolls.

Two ordinary dolls: one boy, one girl. They were old, and their clothing was faded. The girl doll's hair was falling out just above her forehead. The boy doll didn't have any hair at all. . . . just plastic that was colored brown to *look* like wavy hair.

As you can imagine, we were disappointed. And I don't know why I decided to take the dolls home. Maybe I was just curious, and I thought that maybe the dolls were worth some money.

170

But something happened as soon as I got the dolls home.

Something strange.

Soon . . . *very* soon . . . Spencer and I would both be wishing that we'd *never* found those dolls!

2

It started to rain on the way home.

"Great," Spencer groaned. "There goes my day of fishing."

"Well, we didn't find very many worms in the first place," I said.

"Yeah. Too bad I can't fish with dolls."

It didn't rain very hard, but by the time we got home, Spencer and I were soaked. I had held the dolls close, so they didn't get very wet at all.

Mom was in the kitchen when we walked in the door. Rufus, our brown and white cocker spaniel, ran around our feet. Rufus is a great dog, and he's really friendly.

"Look what we found buried in the ground!" I exclaimed, holding up the dolls for Mom to see.

"Make sure you both take your shoes off," Mom said, ignoring the dolls. "They're full of mud."

I kicked off my shoes and pulled my wet hair back away from my face.

"But look at these *dolls*," I said, as I walked into the kitchen. "We found them buried in the ground in an old box."

Mom looked at the dolls. "Are you sure you weren't digging in some old garbage dump?" she asked.

"No," I replied, shaking my head. "We were out in the woods digging for worms. We came across an old box in the ground. When we opened it up, we found these two dolls inside."

"Well, someone probably threw them away," Mom said. She looked me up and down. "Good grief, Serena! You're soaked! Get out of those wet clothes before you catch a cold!"

I walked through the kitchen and into the living room, where I placed the two dolls on the couch. Then I walked down the hall and into my bedroom, changed into dry pants and a shirt, then carried the wet clothing into the bathroom and hung them over the shower curtain rod to dry.

I went back to the living room to get the dolls. My plan was to take them into the garage and clean them up.

But when I went to the couch, one of the dolls was missing!

"Spencer!" I called down the hall. He's always playing tricks on me and trying to scare me. I thought that maybe he hid the doll just to make me mad.

Spencer's head appeared from his bedroom door.

"What?"

"Did you do something with the boy doll?"

He shook his head. "No. I've been in my bedroom. Ask Mom." He disappeared.

I walked into the kitchen.

"Mom . . . have you seen my doll? The boy doll is missing."

"I've been in the kitchen," she said. "Didn't you just have it?"

"Yeah," I said. "But I put both of them on the couch. One of them is missing."

"I haven't seen it," Mom said.

This is too weird, I thought. *How can a doll just disappear? It couldn't have just got up and walked away!*

Well, I was about to find the doll, all right.

And I was also about to find out something else.

The dolls we had found weren't just ordinary dolls.

In fact, they were terrifying.

Terrifying . . . and *dangerous.*

Something caught my eye outdoors.

Something that moved.

And when I saw what it was, I gasped in terror.

3

The doll was outside . . . and it was being carried by our cocker spaniel, Rufus! He must have picked it up off the couch and took it outside. We have a 'doggie door' on our back door. It allows Rufus to go in and out when he wants.

"Oh, no!" I cried, and ran for the back door. Rufus will sometimes chew things up, and I didn't want him ruining the doll.

I threw open the back door.

"Rufus!" I shouted sternly. *"Get in here! Right now!"*

When he heard me shouting at him, Rufus looked at me sheepishly. He knew that he'd been caught, and he hung his head as he slowly walked toward me. When he reached the door, he dropped the doll on the porch.

"Good boy," I said, petting him on the head. It's hard to stay mad at Rufus. He really *is* a good dog, it's just that he likes to play a lot . . . and he likes to chew on things.

He wagged his tail and scampered out into the yard. I noticed that it had finally stopped raining, too, which was a good thing. The doll would have been soaked by now.

I picked it up. Thankfully, Rufus hadn't started chewing on it, and the doll wasn't damaged.

It was then that I really took a good look at the doll's face.

And the first word that came to my mind was . . . *creepy.*

I don't know why. It just seemed weird. Like it was almost alive or something. It didn't look like any other doll I had ever seen before in my life.

I carried it back through the kitchen where Mom was busy making a cake for the church bake sale. In the living room, the girl doll was right where I had left her on the couch.

I put down the smaller doll and picked up the girl doll. Again, I was struck by how eerie the face looked. There was something about these dolls that wasn't right . . . but I didn't know what it was.

Then, something happened that was more than creepy.

It was more than terrifying.

While I was holding up the girl doll, staring curiously into her face . . . *she winked at me!*

4

I dropped the doll onto the couch and screamed. Instantly, Mom was at my side.

"What's wrong?!" she asked.

"The doll!" I replied in shock. "It . . . it winked at me!"

"Don't be silly," Mom said. She reached down and picked up the doll. I took a step back.

"There's the reason it winked at you," she said. "The eyes move by themselves."

I peered closer and looked. Sure enough, the doll's eyelid closed when she was leaned backward.

"But . . . but she didn't have those kind of eyelids before!" I stammered. "She didn't!"

"Of course she did," Mom said. She handed me the doll. "I tell you, Serena. You have quite an imagination."

Mom didn't believe me!

I stared at the doll. Now it creeped me out even more. I just knew that something wasn't right about these dolls.

Why would someone go through the trouble to put the dolls in a box and bury them in ground? I wondered. It just didn't make sense.

Unless, of course, someone was trying to get rid of the dolls for some reason. They wanted to put them someplace where no one would find them.

Or perhaps in a place where the dolls couldn't get out.

Don't be goofy, I told myself. *Dolls are dolls. Besides . . . they might be worth a lot of money.*

We live in ??????? Delaware. There's a really cool collectible store that has all kinds of different things like coins, stamps, old bottles . . . stuff like that. I wanted to take the dolls there to show the store owner. Maybe they would know something more about them.

However, that wasn't going to happen. Not today, anyway. Mom asked me to help her in the kitchen, and I spent the rest of the day cooking and baking with her. Spencer went fishing, but he didn't catch anything.

All in all, the day was pretty normal.

The night, however, was going to be anything but normal.

And it was all because of—you guessed it—those two dolls.

You see, I was about to find out that I was right.

Those two dolls weren't ordinary dolls at all. And if you get spooked easily, you're probably not going to want to go any farther.

Stop reading now. I mean it.

Because what was about to happen that night after I went to bed still freaks me out to this very day . . . .

5

Dad came home from work and he brought pizza, which was cool. Mom said she was tired from baking and cooking all day, so Dad picked up two pizzas. Then we all watched a movie on television.

Finally, it was time for bed. I had just pulled the covers back when Mom called out to me.

"Serena . . . come get your dolls and put them away."

To tell you the truth, I had forgotten about the two dolls. I had put them on a bookshelf in the living room where Rufus couldn't get at them.

I went out and took them from the shelf. Then I walked back into my bedroom and put the dolls on my dresser and climbed into bed. A few minutes later, Mom came in, kissed me on the forehead, turned my bedroom light off, and left. Sometimes Mom lets me read in bed before I go to sleep, but tonight I was too tired.

However, as soon as all of the lights in the house went out, I realized that I would never get to sleep with those creepy dolls staring at me. I could see their dark silhouettes, and even their eyes and facial features. They looked even spookier than before.

Staring at me.

I closed my eyes and tried to forget about the dolls, but it was impossible. Have you ever felt like someone was watching you? That's exactly what I felt like. I felt like I was being spied on.

Finally, after a few more minutes of trying to get to sleep, I slipped out of bed and walked to the dresser. I picked up both dolls, opened up my closet door, and tossed them inside. I couldn't see inside the closet, and I didn't care. I just wanted those dolls out of my sight.

I closed the door and climbed back into bed.

And fell asleep.

But not for long.

I must have just fallen asleep when I was awakened by a sound.

A scraping noise.

I pulled the sheets up to my chin, trembling with fear. Because I knew where the sounds were coming from.

My closet.

Then —

A voice!

A child's voice began speaking! And as I listened, my horror ballooned into all-out terror.

"We're coming for you, Serena! We're coming for you . . . ."

FUN FACTS ABOUT PENNSYLVANIA:

State Capitol: Harrisburg

State Nickname: Keystone State

State Animal: White-Tailed Deer

State Bird: Ruffed Grouse

State Motto: "Virtue, Liberty, and Independence"

State Tree: Eastern Hemlock

State Song: "Pennsylvania"

State Flower: Mountain Laurel

Statehood: December 12th, 1787 (2nd state)

FAMOUS PENNSYLVANIANS!

Louisa May Alcott, author

Bill Cosby, actor

Jimmy and Tommy Dorsey, band leaders

W.C. Fields, comedian

Reggie Jackson, baseball player

Gene Kelly, actor and dancer

Tara Lipinski, figure skater

George C. Marshall, five-star general

John Updike, author

Betsy Ross, flagmaker

among many, many more!

GHOST IN THE GRAVEYARD

About the author

Johnathan Rand is the author of the best-selling **'Chillers'** series, now with over 1,000,000 copies in print. In addition to the **'Chillers'** series, Rand is also the author of **'Ghost in the Graveyard'**, a collection of thrilling, original short stories featuring *The Adventure Club.* (And don't forget to check out **www.ghostinthegraveyard.com** and read an **entire story** from 'Ghost in the Graveyard' *FREE!*) When Mr. Rand and his wife are not traveling to schools and book signings, they live in a small town in northern lower Michigan with their two dogs, Abby and Salty. He still writes all of his books in the wee hours of the morning, and still submits all manuscripts by mail. He is currently working on his newest series, entitled **'American Chillers'**. His popular website features hundreds of photographs, stories, and art work. Visit:

WWW.AMERICANCHILLERS.COM

Join the official

AMERICAN CHILLERS

FAN CLUB!

Visit www.americanchillers.com for details

NEW!
AMERICAN CHILLERS
PICTURE PAGES!

With good friend Adam Rose at Camp Quality!

AMERICAN CHILLERS PICTURE PAGE!

Johnathan and Mrs. Rand, along with a bony friend
at Hubbardston Elementary!

AMERICAN CHILLERS PICTURE PAGE!

A live teleconference with other schools over the internet!

AMERICAN CHILLERS PICTURE PAGE!

Question and answer session at Way Elementary!

AMERICAN CHILLERS
PICTURE PAGE!

With Mrs. Rand at Summer Scream at Clark's Ice Cream and Yogurt, Berkley, Michigan, home of the best ice cream in the WORLD!

AMERICAN CHILLERS
PICTURE PAGE!

Some friends at Pine Lake Elementary!

AMERICAN CHILLERS PICTURE PAGE!

Being interviewed by a fan!

AMERICAN CHILLERS
PICTURE PAGE!

See what reading 'American Chillers' does to the
faculty at Patterson Elementary?!?!!

AMERICAN CHILLERS
PICTURE PAGE!

Chillin' with the gang at Cheyenne Elementary!

AMERICAN CHILLERS PICTURE PAGE!

Scaring up some fun at Clinton Valley Elementary!

AMERICAN CHILLERS
PICTURE PAGE!

Taping a television interview!

AMERICAN CHILLERS PICTURE PAGE!

Signing books after a presentation at the
Birmingham Public Library!

For information on personal appearances, motivational speaking engagements, or book signings, write to:

AudioCraft Publishing, Inc.
PO Box 281
Topinabee Island, MI 49791

or call
(231) 238-0297

About the cover art: This unique cover was designed and created by Michigan artists Darrin Brege and Mark Thompson.

Darrin Brege works as an animator by day, and is now applying his talents on the internet, creating various web sites and flash animations. He attended animation school in southern California in the early nineties, and over the years has created original characters and animations for Warner Bros (Space Jam), for Hasbro (Tonka Joe Multimedia line), Universal Pictures (Bullwinkle and Fractured Fairy Tales CD Roms), and Disney. Besides art, he and his wife Karen are improv performers featured weekly at Mark Ridley's Comedy Castle over the last eight years. Improvisational comedy has provided the groundwork for a successful voice over career as well. Darrin has dozens of characters and impersonations in his portfolio. Darrin and Karen have a son named Mick.

Mark Thompson has been a professional illustrator for 25 years. He has applied his talents with toy companies Hasbro and Mattel, along with creating art for automobile companies. His work has been seen from San Diego Seaworld to Kmart stores, as well as the Detroit Tigers and the renowned 'Screams' ice-cream parlor in Hell, Michigan. Mark currently is designing holiday crafts for a local company, as well as doing website design and digital art from his home studio. He loves sci-fi and monster art, and also collects comics for a hobby. He has two boys of his own, and they're BIG Chiller Fans!

All AudioCraft books are proudly printed, bound, and manufactured in the United States of America, utilizing American resources, labor, and materials.

USA